Arrant Press

One Shot

Tom Conyers, an award-winning filmmaker (The Caretaker – 2012), is also a poet, playwright, painter, illustrator and photographer. To check out his other work, including the novel *Forever Human* and *Morse Code for Cats,* please visit his website:

www.tomconyers.com

Will *I* live on as the ghost lives on
  In the house that once stood entire,
When I am dead but my poems are read,
  And reciting returns to the fire?

– *Adelaide Gazette*, Uncredited, Feb 1957

ONE SHOT

Tom Conyers

ONE SHOT

Copyright © Tom Conyers 2014

www.tomconyers.com

Published by Arrant Press

P.O. Box 406, Burwood VIC, Australia 3125

ISBN-10: 0980587131

ISBN-13: 978-0980587135

Edited by Bryony Sutherland

Cover Design by BrightSpark

Photographs by Tom Conyers

They listen for hours. Nothing except the sounds of cockatoos and kookaburras. They open the trapdoor and peep out. They have judged it well: dusk. Their eyes wouldn't have coped with full daylight, having been a month in the cellar. Rex looks around for the dogs. He can see mounds in the grass. Hauling surviving bitch, Soldier, up the ladder, he heads towards the shed.

Kerrie calls after him, voice shaking. 'Where are you going?'

He turns to her. 'To get the generator working.'

'But why would – ?'

'Follow the plan,' he cuts her off harshly. Then: 'Kerrie?'

She stops. 'Yes?'

There is nothing he can think to say.

In the house, no electricity, no gas. Kerrie's hands tremble on the telephone – not even a dial tone. She knew this would be the case.

The drawers, the cupboards – everything has been rifled through. Her home.

In the shed, Rex is lucky to find two cans of petrol that weren't taken, unseen under a mouldy rug. He fuels the generator.

Once the tank-water is hot enough, they shower in silence, barely touching. When Kerrie steps out, Rex calls Soldier in. Tail between legs, she submits, squirming afterwards on the bathmat as he vigorously towels her, her itches and irritations washed away with a month's worth of grime.

Rex gets dressed then sits down next to the television. Soldier slumps beside him, owner-fixated like a typical blue heeler. Rex stares at the blank screen. The fact the television wasn't stolen makes disturbing sense – only basic survival items have gone. He senses Kerrie watching him from the bedroom doorway. He turns on the TV. The set-top box works to find a channel. White noise.

Kerrie bites back a sob and disappears through the bedroom door, shutting it behind her.

Rex heads to the kitchen and grabs a beer, quickly closing the door on the putrid smell emitting from the fridge. On the fridge door, his cherished photos of the surrounding scrub: an old rusted Holden, peppered with shot; a hand-sawn fence, his dogs crawling under its lowest plank on their bellies; a plain of dust, with whirly-gigs patrolling it like sentries. He swallows. If they can't find help, they're in the middle of nowhere.

He returns to the TV. If, somewhere, someone has survived, the dish on the roof will pick them up. Their house used to belong to the army general from the nearby military base. Rex will search for signals further afield than Australia. No need to panic yet.

Kerrie keeps peeping out of the bedroom to see how he is doing. The same white noise. He doesn't know what to say to comfort her. This is shaping up as even worse than they feared. The very worst.

This night seems longer than those spent in the cellar. Because tonight they have heard how the rest of the world has fared: in thundering, echoing silence. Through their bedroom door, he can hear Kerrie crying one moment, silent the next. Then her screams. He enters the room and lies down behind her, making two 'S's'.

'Wake up, wake up,' she is telling herself.

Near dawn, he and Soldier investigate those two mounds outside. He can only tell by the collar that one of them is his dog, Roger. He's pretty sure the second shape is his other dog, Buzz. No collar, though. Soldier sniffs them, then paws at what's left of their bodies. Rex fights tears. There are also a few human limbs scattered about, gnawed down to the bone. Everything is a dark blue.

Back inside, he and Soldier watch the sunlight rise up the walls like an incoming tide. He glances over at the bedroom door. No sound, which hopefully means Kerrie's getting some sleep. Shifting to the carpet in front of the TV, with Soldier following, he tries to get a signal once more. The static resolves to a picture. A news broadcast, played on a loop. A woman talks directly to camera, lines of fear etched on her face.

He can't take it in. He watches the broadcast twenty times. On the twenty-first, he cranks up the volume. The bedroom door opens almost instantly. Kerrie watches the television as Rex watches her.

'This is our last broadcast,' says the presenter in her earnest English accent. 'We have found the source of the contagion: water. Whatever you do, don't consume any unsealed bottles of water. Goodbye and good luck.'

The woman gives her viewers one last crumpled smile before the warning replays itself.

'This is our last broadcast. We have found the source of the –'

Rex turns it off. Kerrie remains perfectly still.

'I'm sorry, Kerrie,' he says.

She says nothing.

He opens his last bottle of beer, hearing the hiss as

4

the reason he's survived, and raises it in a grim toast.

Bottled drinks – that's all they'd consumed down in the cellar. And for him, most of that had been booze. They hadn't had time to connect a supply to the rainwater tank –luckily, as it turns out. And luckily neither of them had drunk the water under the shower yesterday evening. Warm water – ugh! Or would they turn out to be fortunate after all?

He waves his bottle at Kerrie again. She shakes her head.

He drains the beer in three quick gulps. When he casts his eyes down, he realises he has lost sight of her.

She looms over his shoulder, glass in hand.

'You should drink water for a change,' she says, voice unnatural, robotic.

'I don't like water,' says Rex on autopilot. 'I don't like the taste.'

Throwing her head back, Kerrie empties her glass, the water running down her throat, both inside and out.

The thought 'glass' floats through Rex's pickled brain. A second later, the glass falls from Kerrie's fingers, bouncing on the carpet. Rex only then realises: she's drunk the water, the water from the tap.

'Kerrie ...?'

Soldier springs to her feet, teeth bared. Rex reaches for Roger's collar, washed and resting on the

TV set, as Kerrie leaps at him. 10:00am.

Twenty-four hours later. The film *Solaris* cuts out halfway through. The fuel has run out in the generator. No more electricity, which means no CDs or DVDs to distract him. Just the house and Soldier, both sighing expectantly, both watching to see what he will do next. There *is* no next. In the cellar, he and Kerrie could still hope to emerge and find the world recovered. *This* is next. He screams.

Soldier returns to his side. Unseeing in his agony, Rex gropes forward and pats her wiry head. Finally raising himself from the carpet, he heads outside, shutting Soldier safely indoors. She scratches at the door and whines. He makes his way under the veranda to the kitchen side of the house. The close December heat and light smother him. Stealing himself against the nausea, Rex is still knocked to his knees by the sight of his girlfriend chained to the hills hoist in the middle of their lawn, the grass blotched yellow where his three dogs used to cock their legs or crouch to piss. Kerrie strains, ropey strings of bloody saliva dangling obscenely from her chin. She has entangled herself in the chain. The rusty links cut a shadow chain of blue and purple round her neck. Her bared teeth are bordered in blood; her eyes, framed red. She thrusts out clawed hands as her teeth chomp down on air.

How could she have left him like this?

'Oh God, oh God.'

The cockatoos and kookaburras squawk and cackle in the blue gum trees. Soldier barks a warning at the kitchen window where she's jumped up. Kerrie's mouth opens slackly. Rex's heart bloats with such pain he must turn away. How could she drink the water? She's left him ... with a monster.

Back inside, his eyes pass over the water puddle around the bowl on the linoleum floor ... Soldier's drunk from it? Who filled it? Could only have been Kerrie when they emerged from the cellar. And she could only have filled it with tap water; they'd run out of bottled water in the cellar. That's what had eventually forced them out.

It's in the water. The virus is in the water.

Soldier ogles him. He thinks about the fact that Soldier has drunk the water and seems okay.

Dogs are immune.

This gives him some hope but it seems flimsy.

The sound of the kookaburras' cackling resonates from outside. Rex peers out the window to see two cockatoos sitting happily in a hanging pot of purplish succulent. Presumably the cockatoos have drunk the same water that filled their tank?

The virus must just affect humans.

Rex shifts his eyes from the cockatoos to Kerrie on her knees in the middle of the lawn, her head swaying. His heart swells, partly with grief, partly anger. She peers up, seemingly straight at him. But how can she see him? From the outside, the widow must be a square of light. Is she Kerrie? Is this Kerrie? She staggers to her feet. The crests of the cockatoos open like flick-knives. They flap away, stained hankies, as Kerrie runs straight at the window. The chain yanks her flat. She slavers on the ground, teeth gnashing and rending air.

'Oh God.'

He must end this.

In the lounge, his eyes rest on the sword displayed above the door. Soldier, dropping on the ground, scrutinises him. Rex climbs on a steamed-wood chair Kerrie's mother gave them and carefully takes the sword down. Two-handed, heavy, with a blade over half his height, its edges have never been sharpened, its point never pointy. He takes it outside, shutting Soldier in with difficulty; she's becoming adept at ducking through. More than ever, she doesn't want to be left alone. Rex empathises.

In the shed, he searches for a file. The lathe would be faster but he doesn't have that choice. He finds a metal file and sets about sharpening the blade. He wants to do it in one swing.

Kerrie never liked the sword. He was ambivalent about it himself but only because he thought he'd bought one in the traditional Spanish style and yet, when he got home from Toledo and the sword finally arrived by ship, taking a gander at the haft, he discovered the inscription: 'Robin of Sherwood'. Maybe the guy he'd bought it from swapped it. Rex was sure he'd picked a different one.

But that's not why Kerrie hated the sword. In her opinion, it was too juvenile.

Thinking of Kerrie like that, even of Kerrie in disapproval-mode, his sight blurs out of focus with tears and he accidentally files one of his fingers; a dot drawing of blood. He must get this over with. He wipes his eyes on the sleeve of his white shirt and redoubles his work, brow perspiring. How could she leave him alone like this?

Thirsty. Sharpening the blade has made him thirsty. Deeply, ravenously parched. All he's drunk in the last week is alcohol and, in the last twenty-four hours, nothing.

He steps outside the shed. Kerrie bites and snarls, the collar cutting her neck with her hunger to eat him. That's exactly what she wants to do. She doesn't so much as blink her pitted eyes at Soldier; even though the dog stands on the kitchen bench, barking through the window. This … *thing* is not interested in canine flesh. The horror and ghastliness of it wells up within him. He must get this over with.

Rex assumes the stance then closes his eyes as Kerrie strains towards him. He has practiced this swing in the shed.

2:00pm. Numb. He must be in shock. He barely feels anything. He heads to the west side of the house. From the smell and hiss, the barbecue still has gas in the bottle. He boils a pot of tank water. While he waits for the water to cool, he fetches from the cellar three plastic bottles – two emptied ginger beer and one Coke container he'd used as mixers for his spirits. Filling the plastic bottles via a funnel, he screws on all their lids bar one. He hears Kerrie moaning, her voice carrying over the rusted corrugated roof. At the last second, his resolved failed him.

He wonders if he will remember her as she is now, if he has much time left to remember himself. He's had dogs put down and does not think of them sinking into his arms as they sank into death. He recalls them as alive, their snouts in his lap, their oily black eyes only for him.

Thirsty.

Taking the unlidded bottle inside, Soldier jumps up, her ears flat to her head. He gently pushes her away with a knee and heads into the kitchen. He lifts the bottle to his mouth. Too hot to drink? He can't wait. Soldier watches his every move. The threaded plastic touches his lower lip.

He lowers the bottle and turns to the TV.

'Boiled water!' he curses. 'You didn't say if you could drink boiled water!'

10

But the TV is dead.

3:00pm. A fat huntsman edges out from behind a picture of Kerrie's niece, a hand feeling for a light switch.

Soldier watches Rex from the kitchen where she's been lurking. He gets up from the couch and goes into the bedroom. The sheets are disturbed from Kerrie tossing and turning all night. The last time he'd ever sleep alongside her. Alone. Soldier walks in and leans on his leg. Not quite alone. He lies down. Feeling the empty space beside him too keenly, he calls Soldier. She jumps from the foot of the bed to lie beside him. As tears roll down his cheeks he wonders how his body can possibly have any moisture to spare. His dreams of Kerrie are crowded out by images of streams, rivers, lakes – *water*.

Eventually he wakes, even thirstier. He must find water or collapse. And there is no one now to pick him up. He's used up his fuel barrels on the generator. He hopes he has enough petrol left in the car. He panics afresh with a new worry. Does he still have his car? Did the thieves leave it?

They've taken Kerrie's up-to-date black coupé but left his old bomb. The out-dated maroon Toyota Cressida may prove a blessing. A new car he wouldn't have a hope of servicing, not with the way they are plugged into computers these days – *were*.

Everything is past tense. He loads the boot with the few useful items the scavengers left. Leaving the carport, he fills a bowl of water, puts it on the ground near Kerrie, and pushes it the rest of the way with a broom along the bumpy, dead grass. She knocks it over trying to claw at him and Rex recoils as a small stream trickles towards him. But then, he and Kerrie showered in the contaminated water, didn't they? He's safe so long as it doesn't get in his mouth.

His situation is still futile, though.

'Help me,' he sobs.

Kerrie snarls.

He returns to the car, where he's left Soldier so that she wouldn't attack Kerrie. No sooner had his girlfriend downed the fatal glass of water, than his dog's reaction to her changed instantly. Maybe it's her smell, maybe her stance – Rex doesn't know. But Soldier has been on the defensive ever since, her hackles rising whenever she comes within a wall's distance of the thing that remains.

He starts up the Cressida, the sword on the back seat, Soldier in the front passenger seat, Kerrie's spot. He tries to stop himself from licking his lips; they will only crack the more. His mouth feels like the recipient of a vacuum cleaner's contents. Water.

His skin prickles all over. Not just emotionally but physically: he's gravely, gravely ill.

The town lies half an hour away. Along the road, a pram, sky-blue as if cut out of the background, which he doesn't want to stop and peer into. Several cars broken down which he doesn't bother to check. He should. He only has half a tank.

He examines Soldier. Normally she'd have her head out the window. But she isn't quite the same dog after the horrors of the last month. She pined for Buzz and Roger, found the time in the cellar a claustrophobic madness, and seemed to instantaneously forget the old Kerrie. There's not much joy left for Soldier now.

The Cressida picks up speed and Soldier unexpectedly thrusts her body half out the window. This is more like her. In the wind, the folds of her lips ripple like fins on a manta ray. She is the only dog he's owned who unmistakably smiles. He doesn't doubt that all dogs smile, but with her, even her cheeks dimple. She is smiling now, her head jerking in the direction of the sandy rabbits darting past.

So rabbits are unaffected as well?

Soldier turns and smiles at him. Rex feels a stab of grief.

He squints at the road ahead, the sun de-saturating the desert colours to a sepia print. To his right, the three metre high fence with razor wire and spaced signs whizzes past: 'American Military Zone – Keep Out'. The place where Kerrie worked, where he never visited because he wasn't allowed …

Just what had they done?

Rex slows down. Soldier pulls her snout into the

13

car. Ahead, the town: flat as the desert, struggling to raise its head above dust and scrub. A few wispy clouds, barely written on the sky. It used to be that clouds signalled hope, sagging bellies the promise of rain. Especially out here. But now it's in the water. The virus is in the water … Kerrie's face, contorting as it took over …

Crash. Rex thuds into his steering wheel. Soldier yelps.

Two shoes are hanging over a wire of a telegraph pole, their shoelaces tied together. He waits for them to pass. They don't. A bead of moisture trickles onto his top lip and he licks at it thirstily. Tastes like iron. He dabs at it then contemplates his fingers. Blood.

He's run off the road.

'Soldier.'

She jumps through the window, landing on the seat beside him. Good, she couldn't have been hurt to still move like that.

Did he lose concentration? Pass out? The latter. Water, he needs water. He's a husk of body, drawing on itself for a drop. A humpless camel. He turns the key in the ignition. Thank God, the car restarts. He backs away from the wooden pole and onto the scalded road, hoping the car is facing the right way. He knows this stretch intimately, but right now both directions appear the same.

He turns to Soldier and she blurs into three-headed Cerberus. He fixes the bitumen in sight and decides to drive down the middle; at the moment, it's mimicking a ten-lane highway. Yes, if he doesn't drink soon, when he passes out a second time, he may not wake.

He slows down to forty on entering the town. Old habits. A corpse in the main street, fallen between two angled cars, its extremities chewed off. Impossible to recognise. Though new to the area, Rex knew the locals, at least in passing. There is rubbish in the street. Most of the windows are broken.

Rex barely has spit to swallow. He enters the general store, lurching like a drunk and just as dehydrated, Soldier for once keeping her distance. Thirst.

From the look of the splintered planks, the store was boarded up. Barricaded, maybe. Perhaps someone rammed a car to get inside. Another corpse lies on the ground with the familiar shape of the owner, Mike. Intact. Not even chewed. There are bullet holes in the walls, so maybe he died that way.

Rex trembles. Just what havoc did neighbour wreak on neighbour? Without hope, staggering, he searches for supplies. All the fridges are empty, the food missing from the toppled-over shelves. Nothing. He and Kerrie were a month in hiding, so he knows in his heart that every town from here to Melbourne will have been ransacked by the survivors. In their cellar, several times he and Kerrie heard the locals above, trying to break in. The story must have got out about Kerrie buying up nearly every item in the general store. Her Corolla skidded to a stop at their house, a parachute of dust. Hopping out, she told him they had to get into their cellar. Wait it out.

'Wait what out?'

She wouldn't say. They unloaded the car of food and bottled water, and the copious amounts of alcohol she'd also bought.

He'd wanted to open the trapdoor one time – Gus called out, the only local he'd really made friends with –but she clawed at him and they toppled over. A shot, punctuated with a beam of light, spat up the slate floor at their feet. A few shrieks and many more shots broke the wood of the trapdoor in the scuffle above. A hand scrabbled for the latch, before it spasmed and fell down onto their floor below, amputated by teeth. Kerrie stopped the hole with a rag she'd poured lighter fluid on, so the creatures could no longer smell her and Rex's scent. 'The Turned' – that's what Kerrie had called them. She and her colleagues must have coined that term.

For the rest of their self-imposed incarceration in the cellar, she wouldn't talk, hulking in a corner, whimpering. Rex hadn't known the meaning of the word inconsolable till he'd seen it in her. In the end, he'd retreated to his own place: booze. Poor Soldier, left in the middle.

He finishes searching the aisles, struggling to focus on even those objects he holds millimetres from his face. Nothing of use, not even a lighter. The only thing that hasn't been rifled through is a cylindrical wire display rack. On it, postcards, several of them displaying his own photographs of 'local spots of natural beauty'. Judging from their abundance, none has been taken. His postcards multiply exponentially before his eyes. Before he knows it, he waltzes the rack to the floor.

With some effort, he pushes the rack off him. It rolls away, scattering the last postcards onto the slate floor with a dry flicker. Soldier lays down beside him, in Sphinx-pose. Her ears prick up. He realises everything now sounds like it's underwater to him. Yet there is a hopeful sound peaking through the muted hum. He makes himself listen.

A car, not running too well from the sounds of it. Climbing to his feet feels like climbing to a peak. Keeping in the shadow, he edges towards the door, just in time to see a tan vehicle disappear round the side of the building. He hears it roll to a stop and the engine turn off.

He waits for the occupant or occupants to enter, preparing his smile. He loses his smile at a thought. Whoever they are, they'll be in desperate need of water themselves. They won't be sparing any for him. Did he and Kerrie open their cellar trapdoor?

Oh God, oh God.

His heart leaps at the slamming of two doors, one momentarily after the other like the blast and echoing crack of a rifle being discharged.

'Stay,' he croaks at Soldier, his mouth so dry he can barely make the sound.

He ambles to his car, placing his palm on the bonnet – still warm. But so is the sun; perhaps the vehicle's occupants won't guess he's here. He reaches through the left-rear window, grabbing one of the bottles of boiled water. He hurries inside, nearly losing his balance, and places the bottle in the empty drinks fridge before finding a hiding spot behind an overturned plastic table. He can hear the sound of boots on gravel outside. What if they take his car, with theirs sounding so clapped-out? His sword – no, he's left it lying on the counter! Too late to get it, he sinks back down behind the table and holds Soldier close.

A handgun, which Rex recognises from the movies is a Colt Python, enters the smashed door first. It is attached to a golden-haired, sunburnt arm. This leads to a grizzled, bearded man – gaunt, upsettingly gaunt. Rex steals himself. The man is his age, mid-thirties, perhaps slightly older. Rex's heart contracts yet further when he sees what the man holds in his other arm, the hand of a freckled, auburn-haired boy. The child also has sunken cheeks. His lips are cracked but not as badly as the man's. Has the man given the boy the greater portion of their water? The two barely react to the dead storeowner. The things they must have seen. People have fought and suffered while he and Kerrie exhausted their stockpile of food and water in relative safety underground. The kid finds the bottle in the warm fridge.

Rex stifles a cry. What is he doing? Why did he put it there? His thirst hasn't just gotten the better of him: it has become him. His single, pressing thought. This is why, calculatedly, he put it there: he must know if boiling the water neutralises the contagion.

'Dad, here.'

'Wait, Son.'

The father gently takes the bottle from his son's hands. Holding it up to his ear, he turns the lid. There is no plastic tear.

'It's not sealed,' says the father, his voice barely mustering disappointment. Rex breathes out in relief.

'I'm so thirsty, Dad.'

'I know, Son.'

'We'll die.'

'We'll find water. Whoever ransacked this place, didn't take that water so maybe we shouldn't.'

The father places the bottle on the worn, laminate counter with its chipboard showing through, glances at the sword with a moment's curiosity, then makes his way into the back of the shop, telling the boy to keep searching. The door shuts behind him.

The kid lifts up the bottle. Rex tries to make a sound of warning. It won't issue because he won't

19

last another day without water; he must know. He thinks of the tests Kerrie must have done at her work, the military base, the … The kid steals a sip.

Rex has only observed the change once. Kerrie's veins popped out red and blue, the thumbprints of purple under her eyes darkened, her lips rolled back like a busted stem, and the light in her eyes winked out. She 'turned' in less than half a minute.

The kid seems okay. He wants to drink the whole bottle but he puts the lid on it and places it on the counter. He smiles and hurries out the back. Probably to tell his father the good news. The door slams shut in the wind-tunnel created by the smashed shop-front.

'Thank God,' cries Rex with dry tears. 'Thank God.'

He staggers to his feet. Unlike the boy, Rex cannot wait, heading straight for the water. He'll give the father and son the two bottles in the car. He twists off the lid and lifts it to his mouth. About to tip it back, the door crashes open. The father falls backwards into the room, his son on top of him like a feral, ginger cat. Soldier snarls. The kid bites into his father's arm as his father shoots his son in the eye. Soldier stops barking with a gasp. An umbrella of blood and brain briefly opens from the back of the boy's head before collapsing. The father, splattered with blood, stares at his torn arm then up at Rex standing over him. Rex puts the bottle on the counter. The father gently pushes off his son, rises to a kneeling position, and proffers his gun to Rex.

'Shoot me. I'm next.'

Rex takes the gun. Strange pulses and twitches distort the father's face and body. Soldier resumes her growl. Rex holds the gun at the man's rippling forehead but hesitates.

'How many bullets left?' he asks.

The father draws moist eyes from his son, the last image he wanted to be left with.

'What ...?' he asks, confused. 'One shot.'

Stonily, Rex puts the gun on the counter. The father realises his mistake. Rex grabs the sword and swings just as the father turns and leaps at him. The father falls down next to his son, half-beheaded.

12:00pm. Rex sits on the floor, back to the counter. The grimy slate is still cool from the night. He regards the Colt Python six-shooter he is holding in his lap. It idly occurs to him that it is heavier than he imagined a handgun to be. Soldier tentatively licks the drying blood of the father and son. She might as well, he thinks – she's obviously immune. Light blows in like a curtain from outside. Flies swarm round the two recent dead – the shop owner has been dead too long to warrant a fresh cloud. Their buzzing drills into Rex's head. He cleans the gun carefully before pushing its barrel towards his tonsils. Gagging, he aims it at the roof of his mouth instead. That's how it's done, isn't it? Soldier intelligently stares at him, head keeled to one side. He removes the barrel. He can't leave her like that.

He needs two shots. Two.

Quiet. Not even the hum of a fridge. Just the bzzz of flies. He lies on his side.

Something catches his eye. Under the pilfered drinks fridge, a glint of plastic. Rex sits up, letting out an inhuman noise which garners a quizzical stare from Soldier. He shuffles over, bends down and reaches far under the fridge. A 1.5 litre Coke bottle. He lets out another cry. It must have dropped and rolled under some time back, overlooked by the marauders. He uses his shirt to wipe the dust and grease from the lid, which hisses when he opens it. A breath of bubbles rushes up its sides, a breath of exhalation imitating his own. Even warm Coke feels wonderful cascading down his parched throat. He finishes and immediately gets hiccups, great heaving hiccups like sobs.

He had to know about the boiled water.

Outside, he checks the father and son's vehicle. An old make of Land Rover, square in shape. Not the rounded-off edges of the modern type. Maybe they had his same idea about taking a vehicle they could self-service. Rex inspects the boot: two tins of spaghetti 'with added cheese'. Clothes, sentimental items, a family portrait still in its cheap frame, with wife and two more kids. All redheads.

The tins of food disquiet Rex.

Water makes up a high percentage of all living matter. Animal, vegetable. But if not even boiling the water kills the disease, is the disease in everything that wasn't sealed before the outbreak? Does that mean there is a finite supply of food and drink left to him? If so, he's going to die anyway. By finding the Coke, he's merely staved off the inevitable for half a day — a full day at most. He chokes. Everything goes black for what seems an aeon.

Rex opens his eyes to find himself leaning heavily on the Land Rover's blistering bonnet. Something is missing: Soldier. She is so much a part of him, he trembles and scans the street. Nothing. He hurries back inside the general store, almost howling but for want of lubrication.

Soldier is chewing the fingers of the boy. Rex hasn't been able to feed her, or himself, since they emerged from the cellar. Sitting down shakily next to her, he reaches out to rough the hair round her neck. She growls automatically, throat bloodied. He pulls his hand away, and stands up. She waddles up to him, tail wagging guiltily. He's seen her growling at Buzz and Roger when he's fed them bones. But she's never before growled at him. How hunger and thirst and can make a living thing change.

Soldier can eat and drink, but he will die. He feels a rush of envy and cuffs her. The first time he has ever hit a dog. Her tail wags in small arcs like a

23

snake's as she crawls towards him, hurt but ever loyal. He crouches down, feeling a cad. She leans against him, pawing his chest, and he hugs her.

He closes his eyes again because that way none of this might be real. Because when he opens them, there's a tiny chance he might wake up from a nightmare.

Soldier squirms in his embrace.

'Shhh.'

He is hushing his own measly tears, but their saltiness only preserves his grief. He thinks he can hear singing. Birds – hundreds, thousand of birds – singing their respective parts in the choir of nature, no longer having to compete with gaudy human sounds.

This can't be happening. Boiling water is meant to get rid of every possible contaminate it might contain. How is it possible the virus survives this process? Something feels strange in all this. Surreal, even.

Standing up giddily, he gapes through the maw of the shop front, his eyes adjusting painfully to the glare. How far has the contagion spread? England, going from the accent of that news reporter. Such a distance … Everywhere, from the lack of signals – so the globe over? Clouds would carry it, presumably …?

Wait! Scientists somewhere in the world have surely created an antidote! Even now, they are pumping it into lakes and seeding clouds!

But the hope is so Hollywood it cannot settle him beyond a moment.

Rex glances across at the empty plastic shelves behind the counter. What would have been taken from *there*? Then he gets it: cigarettes – not a single packet left. What we all grope for in death: our addictions.

He feels a weight on his leg. Glancing down, Soldier is sitting on his foot; the dog owning the owner. But for how long? Gently pulling his shoe out from under her, he walks outside and gets in the Cressida, Soldier leaping through the window to be next to him. She can leap and he can barely sit up. He parks next to the Land Rover, and struggles out, still hiccupping from the Coke.

Mechanically, Rex pushes a tube into the petrol tank of the Land Rover, places his lips around the other end, and sucks. Soldier backs away in confusion, whining. The petrol needles down the tube. Pulling his mouth away at the last moment and using his thumb to temporarily block the tube, he quickly feeds it into the Cressida's tank. Capillary action taking over, the petrol snakes reassuringly from one vehicle to the next. The father had a pretty full tank. Rex wonders what else he should take. Spark plugs? He opens the Land Rover's bonnet. The spark plugs are even more corroded than his. He tries to think what else. His car's running a little hot. He locates the Land Rover's water tank. He loses his hiccups from what he sees.

There are two straws in it.

Famished, Rex wolfs down the tinned spaghetti, Soldier refusing her share.

Getting into the Corolla, Rex adjusts the rear-view mirror to reflect the two remaining bottles of boiled water on the back seat. Why has he kept them? Soldier can always drink them. Or the car. This second thought almost makes him snigger as he starts up the engine. He backs the Cressida away from the general store, bumping into a Hyundai Excel abandoned in the middle of the street. For a second, he almost stops to leave his number. Soldier regains her perch on the windowsill.

On the road home, a flock of cockatoos erupts in an explosion of yellow and white up ahead. Once he's driven through, they implode, reclaiming the road.

About six months back, his stepbrother told him to check pictures of Chernobyl on the net. Fenced off since the nuclear meltdown, the trees in the streets were as tall as the houses, wolves wandered with impunity, and only the odd gung-ho tourist passed through to takes snaps. Maybe Rex should bring his camera with him on his next outing. What? He shakes his head at his reflection in the rear-view mirror. Who would he be taking photos for? And how would he charge his camera? His mind's drifting again.

Gravel scraping under the left wheels. Dangerously close to the cat's eyes. He swerves back onto the tar.

The road, he must concentrate on the road.

That sign on the cyclone fencing flashes past, to his left now: 'American Military Zone – Keep Out'.

Kerrie.

They'd met three years back, at a mutual friend's barbecue: Gary. Gary was a physicist researching the 'multiverse'; in particular, universes parallel to ours that operated under different laws of physics. It all sounded pretty speculative to Rex – the stuff of science fiction. Fortunately, Gary's barbecues were more down-to-earth.

When Rex arrived, Gary was splashing his beer on the hot plate as an attempt at a marinade. He waved, and Rex couldn't wave back; he was holding the leash to his sheep dog, Roger, with both hands. Rex noted he was the only one there who'd brought his pet.

Several others he didn't know so well were sloshing about in an inflatable baby pool. Roger twisted out of his collar and sniffed everyone's crotch with his long white snout at least once until Rex got him back on the lead. Flushed with embarrassment, Rex managed to score one of the few deck chairs that wasn't wonky and held his place, with Roger between his legs. An esky, two plastic chairs, and another deck chair supported the rest of the circle he found himself in.

A woman he'd intercepted in the corridor when he first arrived, appeared at his side. It half occurred to him to offer his seat when she crouched down next to him. Rex slipped his hand under Roger's collar so he wouldn't sniff her too.

This was Kerrie of Melbourne, her face white and fresh, not sun-tanned and burnt as it would become in the bush. Pouty red lips even redder against her porcelain skin. Short jet-black hair, with a straight fringe above her green/brown eyes. A little weight worn well, not the axial drawing she became.

She didn't look at him, but let him look at her. He tried to tune into the conversation before his staring turned creepy. Roger rested the upper part of his shaggy body on Rex's lap.

'The government doesn't think microbial research is important,' said a woman, wispy blonde hair.

The pudgy guy next to her, whom Rex knew vaguely –Malcolm – weighed in. 'Try getting funding for what Kerrie and I are researching – targeted viruses.' And he winked at Kerrie.

The conversation continued in this vein. There was nothing Rex could contribute, except pats for his dog. A pause eventually came which Kerrie filled. 'Guys, can we *not* talk about research for once?'

The circle turned to observe her. Malcolm was the first to break the stare, and directed his eyes more generally at the group. 'And as for the government giving grants to …'

He didn't finish the sentence; the joke was made. They guffawed, Kerrie along with them. She joined the discussion for a while before finally turning to Rex.

'Well, since we can't get off the topic, what research are *you* in?' she asked.

'I'm not.'

She cocked her head, her fringe levelling like an altimeter. 'How do you know this mob?'

Rex nodded towards Gary at the smoking barbecue. 'I met Gary when I photographed his wedding. Since then, I've photographed the weddings of half the people here.'

Her cheeks dimpled when she smiled.

'Oh, *you* took those photos? Rex?'

'Yes.'

She proffered a hand. Rex, in proffering his own, let go of Roger, who immediately bounded over several people to get to the barbecue. Momentarily ignoring the potential chaos, they shook hands.

'Kerrie,' she introduced herself. 'Your wedding photos … they're different.'

He smiled, keeping half an eye on Roger. 'I try to make them interesting.'

'For you or the client?'

Rex's grin broadened, and he let Roger wholly out of his sights.

'Both,' he answered.

She explained her research. After a while, she stopped. 'You appear confused?'

'I don't understand,' he said. 'Australia is full of introduced species: dogs, cats, sheep, cows – *us*. Why are some foreign species deemed pests and others not? Why be so selective in wiping out poor cane toads and fire ants?'

She expressed disappointment. 'By "us", you mean us *whites*, I presume?'

The 'I presume' was quaint. Her lips had formed the phrase quite delectably.

Rex glanced round to see Gary feeding Roger a chop. Rex turned back to Kerrie and persevered with his argument. 'Some say dingoes aren't even native to Australia – the Aborigines brought them down from Indonesia when our two countries were joined by an isthmus. But if the Aborigines "brought" them, then where did *they* come from?'

She explained, a little defensively, that the line of research she and her colleague were pursuing was superior: make a pest wipe itself out. The old approach was to introduce a new pest that was the natural predator of the established pest, which in most cases would then cause damage of its own.

Rex recited a nursery rhyme he hadn't thought of since he was a kid. 'There was an old woman who swallowed a fly. I don't know why she swallowed a fly, perhaps she'll die!'

Kerrie nodded shyly. Taking up where he left off, she continued the rhyme, an equally distant memory. 'There was an old woman who swallowed a spider, that wriggled and jiggled and tickled inside her. She swallowed the spider to catch the fly...'

The next line they sang together. 'I don't know why she swallowed the fly, perhaps she'll die!'

The others were staring at them, Malcolm the most intently. But as before, the diversion only held them a moment and they returned to their topic.

Roger was resting his upper body on a seated blonde girl Rex didn't know at all, his long paws with their black and white tendrils of hair, resting on either shoulder. He called Roger but she said he was okay; she had two of her own. Rex consoled himself that at least Roger wasn't pissing on things. He'd even pissed on small dogs in the park, much to Rex's embarrassment.

Kerrie waved a hand over his face.

'Yes, I'm sorry.'

'Have you got your camera here?' Kerrie asked.

Rex nodded.

'Feel like taking a photo of me?'

He reached wearily for his bag. It wasn't that she wasn't photogenic. It was just that he'd been hoping to remain 'off-duty'.

'Not here,' she said, when he'd removed the lens cap.

They left, Malcolm watching them with interest.

Rex took the photos at his place, with Roger left outside, whining. They took photos of each other. It was the best, most erotic, first date he'd ever had.

Rex passes the sky-blue pram and turns down his road, a narrow, dusty track. He is glad he is remembering Kerrie this way.

Only in the morning, as they dressed, did he ask the question he couldn't let go. The thing that had kept him up long after that other thing had finally gone down.

'So, how do you "make a pest wipe itself out"?'

She stopped buttoning her blouse.

'You make it develop an insatiable appetite for its own kind.'

Rex gazed down at his unlaced shoes. 'Cannibalism.'

A few barks from Roger at the back door.

'Yes,' she said, proudly. 'The fly the old woman swallows can now be made to eat itself!'

A thundering crash – the slide-door shaking under Roger's assault. Rex regarded Kerrie's startled face.

'Roger was a champion Old English sheep dog,' he explained. 'Until a horse kicked him in the head. The owner was going to put him down with his wits gone. But I took him in.'

Kerrie nodded slowly then stood up, glancing at Rex's camera bag on the chair by the door.

'You'll wipe those photos, won't you?'

Six months later and Rex had moved into her house in Seddon. While walking Roger in the local park one day, they got talking to a guy whose bitch had just pupped. The guy had one left to gift. Kerrie mentioned that Rex, if he had his way, would love a tribe. Walking home, they got the sense the guy was following them.

Very early the next morning, the doorbell rang. By the time they'd pulled on some clothes and answered it, they found a basket with the pup inside, and a nametag: 'Buzz'.

Buzz was the unlikely conjunction of Beagle and Alsatian. The Beagle was most pronounced in her colours: brown, black, a saddle of white on her back, and of course her large, floppy ears. In general shape, she was pure, if slightly diminutive, Alsatian.

'Seems like we're starting a family,' said Kerrie.

Rex squints at the road. With the sun high above, the light is no longer in his eyes, but he's thirsty, hungry, tired, desperate – thirsty. And hot. The breeze coming through the open windows cools him off but also dries his already parched skin. Soldier half jumps out each time she sees a rabbit flash by. Slashes of blue make up the land to the horizon – knives seen edgeways. But they aren't water; they're mirages. And even if they weren't, he couldn't drink from them anyway. Soldier studies him and she is smiling. He sobs and she loses her grin.

Kerrie rises to her feet on the sound of him pulling up. Soldier barks at sight of her. Rex is almost sick when he sees that Kerrie has eaten her left hand down to the wrist where it smokes with flies. Dangerously close to fainting, he leaves Soldier in the car, the window half wound up to stop her from jumping out. He holds the Colt to Kerrie's forehead as she strains on the chain, trying to savage him, the gristle from her own flesh dripping from between her teeth.

This is not Kerrie. This can't be Kerrie. Kerrie left him.

The trigger is hard to pull, something else he hadn't imagined about guns. What does the term 'hair-trigger' mean then? Before he knows it, he fires, the crack hammering in his ears. Blood spurts from her crown as she topples over. Soldier stops barking.

Next to the back porch, he covers her in a mound of bone-white wood, Soldier enjoying the fossicking. He takes comfort in the fact that Soldier takes even less interest in Kerrie now she's dead; this isn't her. He shoves paper in, then lights a match. It doesn't take long to catch and soon the pyre rages, its red competing for brilliance with the sunset. It is the third such mound he's built to cremate loved ones in as many days. There was also Buzz and Roger, once he'd removed Roger's collar.

Buzz and Roger whom the Turned had killed but not eaten. Because the Turned had only wanted to eat him and Kerrie, their own species. Cannibalism.

'Wait what out?' he'd asked, when Kerrie braked outside their house, trailing a parachute of dust.

Hysterical, Kerrie brayed at him to help get the supplies she'd bought downstairs, into the cellar. He'd obeyed, thinking he'd press her further when she calmed down. Soldier, Buzz and Roger watched, curious and a little alarmed, in a triangle formation. They knew something was awry – Buzz didn't even bother them with her deflated basketball. When Rex and Kerrie were nearly finished, the three dogs sat up and turned in unison to face the wattles to the north of their house. Buzz began a low growl, which the other two accompanied at a higher pitch. The hair on their backs rose like fins.

Shaking, Rex called his dogs.

'Forget them!' blared Kerrie, halfway down the ladder.

She reached for Rex's ankle but he moved towards his dogs.

'I can't, Kerrie.'

She let go.

'Buzz, Roger, Soldier. Come here,' he pleaded. Then, his panic getting the better of him: '*Right now!*'

35

The scrub between the trees revolved like turnstyles. Creatures staggered through the gaps: men, women and children but not men, women and children. Slavering, snarling, snapping things. The Turned. Kerrie screamed from the ladder.

They fell upon Buzz and Roger, who managed to savage two of them before Buzz was seemingly swallowed beneath the writhing mass and Roger was ripped apart before his eyes. Rex grabbed Soldier by the collar, pulling her down roughly into the cellar with him.

He fastened the lock just as those hungry hands began to scratch and beat above. Soldier was howling, cowering in a corner, a thin stream of urine puddling round her paws. Rex realised he too was howling. Buzz, Roger.

'Oh God.'

He turned to Kerrie. 'They want to eat us!'

'No,' cried Kerrie from behind a chair. 'They want to eat the dogs! The dogs!'

He yanked her up by the hair, the first time he'd ever handled a woman roughly. A time for firsts. 'Buzz and Roger – they were collateral,' he bellowed into her face. 'Those "people" – they wanted to cannibalise *us*. How did this happen? How did the virus get out?'

Kerrie would not acknowledge him. Sinking to the floor in a crouch, she held her ears and let out a wail.

This is what she left him with.

It is night, the air thrumming with cicadas. The fire has died down, the last logs like red tile mosaics. Rex is sitting on the dirt, leaning against a veranda post, Soldier by his side. His thoughts return inevitably to water. He thinks of the bottles in the car. Or of the equally poisonous – to humans at least – water in the rain tank. He pulls his body up the post with the slowness of a vine and turns to the windowsill where the Colt Python's resting. The gun that is now empty. He scans from it to the dying pyre, the outline of Kerrie's body still faintly visible in the flames.

The pyre's dim light barely diminishes the rainbow of stars above. The immensity of the heavens. Humans were nothing after all.

He feels something at his side and turns. Kerrie. As she presented when they first met. But even whiter. She nods at the discharged Colt then to her burning body in the pyre.

'Thank you, Rex.'

'Does it matter?' he asks.

He is not surprised to see her, having had little to drink in the last couple of days, and before that only alcohol. The Coke sated his thirst only for its sugariness to leach him further. He feels his eyes are sinking into his head.

'You knew it was in the water,' he states more than asks.

She says nothing. She says nothing when the way she killed herself almost killed him too. Flashes of their tussle on the floor overwhelm him. Thinking at first it was playacting, at a time when nothing was funny.

'Kerrie, you have to give me something. If boiling the water doesn't kill the contagion, does that mean if I eat vegetables I will contract the disease from the water in those?'

Kerrie jokes, her eyes still on the fire. 'You could do an experiment.'

'Like I did with that kid?'

She winces.

'We're both scientists now,' he says nastily. 'What should I do, Kerrie? How can boiling the water not be purifying it? How's that possible? Tell me what to do!'

Her next words are bitter, recriminating. 'When my work became top secret, you were glad you no longer had to ask me about it.' He swivels from her to the Colt with its empty barrel.

What an idiot he's been! He should have used the bullet on himself – or on Soldier. Not on this monster. He'd had one shot – one shot.

CHAPTER TWO

Four days since they emerged from the cellar. Where he is going? *Why* he is going? Is he simply driving till he runs out of petrol or passes out and crashes?

6:00am. He stops the car on an escarpment and backs up. Soldier tenses. The ground falls away to their left into thick scrub. Probably a creek at the bottom, at least in winter. Soldier stares at him expectantly, wondering if he is going to turn off the ignition. He does and she leaps out of the open window, yelping with excitement. Her enthusiasm prises the few measly tears from his eyes he has remaining. They can't have much time left together. He totters out of the car the conventional way, using the hot bonnet for support, fingers prickling. He peers over the edge. Yes, he hadn't imagined it. A tree stump, snapped half a metre up. Around it, bushes either ripped or flattened. The slope isn't too steep but it is gravelly, and it will be hard to maintain purchase in his present dizziness. He thinks he can make out a white object peeping through the undergrowth at the bottom, where it has brought in the sky.

He sways in the dry wind.

What is this compulsion to struggle on? Unless he finds drinkable water down there, he'll never have the strength to climb back up. Is that where he wants to die? In a creek bed?

'Soldier.'

She waddles over. He crouches down unsteadily and removes her leather collar, with its council registration tags and his now defunct mobile number etched into a brass disk. The disk also has his name etched in it – also irrelevant? Soldier shakes her head happily and appears pleased. The collar, he suspects, was one of the few additions to her new life she disliked. Not this *new* new life – the brief one before the Turning.

He ditches it as far as his strength allows. At least she can't get caught on something with the collar gone. It raises her chances without him slightly.

'Help me.'

Soldier rubs against him. Trembling, he holds her close. He hugged her before, but never so feverishly and long. She suffers his embrace good-naturedly, despite how hot it evidently makes her feel in the already stifling closeness.

He smells her oily neck. She's why. She's the reason he hasn't quite given up. He doesn't want to leave her the way Kerrie left him.

Using the Cressida's side mirror to stand, he makes his way to the boot and slowly fills a worn Puma bag with tools and items he might need. With the puny strength he has left, he throws this down the embankment where it catches halfway, on a rock. He's committed now.

He begins the slide, Soldier going up and down thrice in the time it takes him. Pushing through the bushes, he sees a small two-tonne delivery truck. The front window is smashed white. Poking his head through the fallen-out side window, no occupants. Worrying. If they survived, they probably took their supplies with them. And that will mean any water. Despite the cargo being dented like a boxer's head and his growing weakness, he manages to prise open the doors without much difficulty. Inside, tinned peeled tomatoes, hundreds of them.

10:00am. He is already sick of tomato juice. He has set up a blanket in a spot partially shaded from the sun by the overarching branches above. There is a trickle of water in the pebbly creek below his feet, so that's Soldier taken care of as far as water is concerned. A scatter of sunlight plays in the ripples like goldfish. Soldier stretches out along his leg and sighs. Just as he's never quite known a dog to so indisputably smile, so too has he never known one to sigh with such expressiveness. But this time it's not a sigh – it's a groan of hunger. Rex spots a mangy rabbit through the dried, frayed grass and growls. Soldier sits up, copying the noise. The rabbit's head turns their way, before bolting.

'Go on.'

Soldier chases it into the bushes then returns to him, grinning.

He tries again. 'Go on – get it!'

She bounds off in the direction of the departed rabbit then back to him until she is simply doing loops. He pats her head.

'Oh God, Soldier, this isn't a game. That was your dinner, Soldier. That was your dinner.'

He regards her stonily. If only it were Buzz who survived.

He closes his eyes.

He hates to have picked between his dogs, even in this hypothetical fashion. But Roger, skittish Roger, would never have had any hope of surviving on his own, let alone without Buzz. Roger would have had less chance than Soldier.

A year and a half after they were 'given' Buzz, he and Kerrie were walking in the park in Seddon, when a hot air balloon descended from above, a fat exclamation mark in the sky. When Roger fled from the whooping of its flame, who had found him? Not Rex. Rex had put up photos in the street, rang The Lost Dogs Home, the RSPCA, the council, other animal shelters. In desperation, he took Buzz back to the park and said, 'Where's Roger?' Buzz took him on a long walk all the way to Ascot Vale. 'This is not a game,' he kept saying to her. 'This isn't an excuse to get out.' She stopped in a non-descript street. Annoyed, he took her home. There'd been no calls on his landline or emails. That evening, he tried Buzz again. She took him to exactly the same spot, so many suburbs away. Taking her more seriously this time, he asked a few passers by, knocked on doors – no one had seen Roger. If he'd been found, surely Rex would have been rung. As with Soldier, Roger's collar had Rex's number on a disk. Then Rex's mobile rang. A man's voice.

'I've got your dog: Rex.'

'Actually, *I'm* Rex. The dog's name is Roger.'

A pause on the mobile.

'Well, I must say he kept looking around when I said Rex.'

'Can I ask where you picked him up?'

The man said two street names. They formed the corner Rex was standing on, where Buzz had brought him twice, where the scent would have died once the man bundled Roger into his car.

'I live five minutes from there,' explained the man. 'I was already late to work this morning so I dropped him off in my backyard. I've only just come home otherwise I would have rung earlier.'

Rex had to check himself. He would've rung a concerned owner immediately. Not waited eight bloody hours.

'You got a pen?' asked the man. 'I'll give you my address.'

'I'll remember it,' said Rex. Then he noticed a bottle shop at the end of one of the streets. 'Do you like wine?'

'Whisky. Green label.'

Rex bristled.

Roger surviving his bolt across all those busy streets between Seddon and Ascot Vale was a miracle. But Buzz following Roger's scent all the way to that corner was like something out of Lassie. Buzz was a remarkable dog. But then again animals are a lot smarter than most humans would like to think. A lot smarter than is convenient.

Rex spends the rest of the day on the blanket, weak and diarrheic. He bathes once or twice downstream, in a glade which at any other time he would have found enchanted, testing his theory that the water won't turn him through touch. It doesn't. Must only work through ingestion, or saliva from the infected getting into the bloodstream, as with that kid biting his father.

Oh God, that kid. He half-consoles himself he had to know. Well, he knows now. Any humans left are doomed.

From time to time, Soldier gets up and potters about. She chews the grass till she throws up. That's what she used to do when he first found her. He tries her with a tin of tomatoes. She makes a spitting gesture. He pours the tin onto the grass tufts she keeps returning to. She crops a little more. Late in the day, with the valley flooded in cool blue shadow, she finds a skink and plays with it.

'For Christ's sake, Soldier, just kill it.'

The lizard drops its tail. He smashes its head with a rock and throws it at her, where it bounces off her snout, a mangled brooch.

She doesn't pick up its crushed body.

'You'll get hungry enough,' he says.

He wants to eat the tail, with its noughts-and-crosses patterning, but remembers just in time. The water in it, the water in all living things. Kerrie and Malcolm's research must have somehow mingled with Gary's forays into the physics of adjoining universes. He leans back and sleeps.

Hungry.

He is with Kerrie in her rental in Seddon. It is nearly two and a half years after they've met; early evening. She's found out by phone call that her and Malcolm's funding has been cut. Coolly, she puts down the receiver and returns to the fridge. Rex watches from where he is sitting, on a metal stool. He makes the appropriate face of sympathy but they both know he's relieved. A virus that makes a 'pest' cannibalise its own kind? Perhaps that made the university Kerrie and Malcolm worked for as nervous as him. He's very, very glad.

Kerrie lifts her head out of the fridge. 'What about fish?' she asks him. 'Can I cook us fish for dinner?'

She's worried he's not getting enough protein in his diet. He rests his elbows on the Formica bench. With his feet, he's secretly stroking Buzz and Roger. 'Kerrie, you know I'm vegetarian,' he banters, trying to assuage her worries.

She slams the fridge door, which only opens again. She pushes it closed more gently then turns back to him. 'Fish aren't really alive, you know.'

He tries to maintain his pleasant demeanour. 'They're alive enough to die.'

He opens his eyes, his stomach empty of the unsatisfying tinned tomatoes he's voided all day. Yawningly empty. It is night but the moon dusts the leaves and rocks and water silver. He can't see the skink he crushed. Soldier must have eaten it. Good, it's a start. Leaning back on his jacket, he can see the silhouette of a tawny frogmouth on a branch above, a goggled pilot in silent reckoning. Soldier is snuggled against him. He's cold, too.

'Oh God.'

He pulls the blanket to her neck and dozes.

He is at his father's café. The morning coffee rush has subsided and his father and two staff are prepping for lunch. Rex gets his dad alone for a moment, in the rear courtyard, where an umbrella tree blocks out what little light filters through the winter clouds. Cold.

'She's lost her job?' his father asks, while weeding round the pond – always working – Buzz and Roger 'helping' through showing an olfactory interest.

Rex nods.

'And *you've* lost your job, too?'

Rex nods again.

His father frowns. 'I thought you were getting heaps of business with all those weddings?'

Rex sits down at the cold marble-top table, saying nothing, the dogs immediately under his feet.

'I see,' says his father after a moment. 'You've thrown it in. And now you both need cash?'

Rex can't nod a third time. His dad forgets the weeds, gently pushing away the dogs, who rise as he takes a seat at the table.

'Son, you're bludging off me. Listen, we can all dream but at the end of the day, everyone has to work.'

'Beginning of the day.'

'What?'

'Unless you do night shift.'

His father sighs. 'Okay, if you're over weddings, can I ask you this: have you tried, really tried, to make it as an arty-farty photographer?'

Rex bristles. 'I've sent countless photos to publications.'

'Yes, but photos *you* wanted to take, I bet. Obviously not photos *they* wanted.'

'Obviously.

'No need to be a smart-arse.' His father stands, the dogs with him; two customers have stepped into the back yard. Could mean a meal.

Food.

Hungry.

'Look,' says his father, 'have you thought maybe you're not cut out for this arty line of work? You know you're always welcome back here. You were the best barista on the street.'

Rex stirs. The sky is tinged a faint pink. Frozen, he welcomes the rising sun he won't welcome once it's fully risen. His stomach grumbles. What he wouldn't do for a hearty breakfast and coffee at his father's café. Soldier kicks at him in her sleep. He is smothering her. He closes his eyes. Kerrie.

It is two months after he visited his dad. He has his laptop open on Kerrie's kitchen table, surfing the net for work. Buzz and Roger have fought for the prime spot at his feet and Buzz has won. Several people are chasing him for wedding photos but he never wants to attend another wedding again. Even his own. Yet making coffee is the only other skill that's ever landed him a job. And he knows you don't find barista work on the net. You've got to know someone. He considers his dad's offer. He can't, he can't. He's good at it; he's even developed a distant, vague rapport with customers, but it isn't what he wants to do.

Making sure he's alone, he retrieves his camera from his camera bag, plugs in the interface cable, and downloads his latest pictures of a disused brick factory he and the dogs have broken into.

Kerrie peers over his shoulder, with the chemically sweet smell of soap and the steaming warmth of a hot shower clinging to her.

He tries to bring up the job-search window but in his haste nearly knocks his camera to the floor. It's too late; Kerrie's seen the screen displaying his photos.

She towels her hair before wrapping it in a makeshift turban. To his surprise, with arms now free, she loops them around his shoulders, pressing her flushed cheek to his stubbly one.

'Just a small break from job-hunting,' he mutters.

She stares at the screen, at the photos he's downloaded.

'You don't have to find work,' she says.

He pulls away to appraise her. 'What?'

'You don't have to sound so disappointed,' she quips. 'Malcolm and I have found an alternative source of funding.'

He constructs a happy countenance.

'In fact, it found us, through a mutual friend of ours, actually.'

Rex cocks his head.

'Gary!' she exclaims. 'You know how we haven't heard from him? Well, he's landed a prime job researching a universe parallel to, but potentially interpenetrating, ours. It functions under a whole different set of mathematics, apparently, that ...'

(*Yes, that's what went wrong*, Rex thinks in his sleep.)

'Anyway, his bosses are funding research in multiple streams. They're offering for me and Malcolm to come and work for them, too ... And the point I meant to make is: you won't need to earn another dollar for the rest of your life.'

'Who, Kerrie?' he asks. 'Who would fund that kind of work?'

She pulls her head away.

'That came out wrong,' he lies. 'I mean, it's quite specialised ... isn't it?'

She's in too high spirits to be angry with him. 'An American company,' she says. 'I've never heard the name before.'

He looks frightened. She mistakes his expression

for something else.

'I know,' she says. 'Another Australian invention that our own government didn't have the foresight or imagination to back. So it's going overseas.'

It isn't what he's thinking.

'We're going to America?' he asks. That isn't what he's thinking either.

'Well, that's the catch, no. Seems they have a research facility here, in the middle of Australia.'

Rex tilts his head questioningly.

'It's sensitive stuff they're working on. Cutting edge physics. Improving fragile environments in a fragile environment. I guess that's why it's in the middle of woop woop. Probably be next to impossible for you to get a job there, anyway. So you may as well pursue your photography.'

He closes his laptop and the job search window he'd finally managed to bring up, and turns to face her. Kerrie suddenly appears vulnerable, like the lost porcelain doll she resembles.

'You *will* join me?' she asks.

He nods. She nibbles on his ear, her hot toothpaste breath tickling the hairs.

Coffee. He can't go back to making coffees all day. Heart-patterns, fern-leaf patterns – all in the way he pours.

'Rex, you can spend the time getting your photography where you want it. Maybe buy a few accessories here in civilisation first, like that tripod you've seen at Ted's.'

He stands up and hugs her. She lets her dressing gown fall. He feels her warm body against his, and is immediately aroused. Buzz and Roger circle round their feet, thinking that Rex standing up might mean a walk.

'That's great news,' he says, and kisses her.

Three weeks after his lacklustre job search, Rex is sitting at a table with Kerrie on Hamilton Island, celebrating with the advance from her new, American funders. (His father is minding Buzz and Roger, no doubt hits in the café courtyard.) Rex and Kerrie covet their food because the currawongs and crows also covet it. The feet of the birds tap and scrape on the empty blue glass tables among the occupied ones. A nearby pool reflects as perfectly as a mirror the stand of palms and white sandy beach behind. The ocean is green, the sky a cloudless blue.

Kerrie is wearing a straw hat, sunglasses, and long white sleeves to protect her frail white skin underneath. He is only wearing board shorts. He gets out his camera and swaps his new telephoto for a prime lens, then walks closer to the pool and takes a photo. He shows it to her on the display screen when he sits back down.

'It's postcard quality,' she says. 'Maybe they'll buy them here,' she adds.

He shakes his head. 'From the gift shops, I think

they've got this place shot from every angle.'

'But you've got an unusual eye.'

They sip their Berry Fabs: cocktails of coconut and cherry liquor, Cointreau, blended berries, chocolate sauce, cream and rum. A truly decadent holiday.

'You're sure you're happy about leaving Melbourne?' she asks, trying to scoop the chocolate coated to the inside of her glass with a straw. She's sensed his unease and put it down to him not wanting to be uprooted from his friends.

'You know I'd follow you anywhere,' he says at last.

By the way her head turns, giving him her profile, she seems disappointed in his answer. She turns to face him again.

'You always joke with me but this is my chance to make an impact. There is no limit to what Malcolm and I can achieve with this research.'

It's his turn to glance away. Malcolm. He is sick of hearing about Malcolm. But all he does is copy Kerrie in scraping the chocolate from his now empty cocktail.

A particularly daring currawong, with its yellow and black eyes like stitched-on buttons, steals a chip from his plate. Chips are one of the few vegetarian options on the island.

Rex's stomach grumbles in his sleep. Food.

Kerrie puts her cocktail glass down and stares across at him. 'If that hotel in Brisbane takes your photos for their brochure, you should insist that you're credited.'

'I don't care about the credit.'

She frowns — is about to say something — but closes her mouth.

She raises her arm to motion the waiter for the bill, but Rex tells her not to worry — they'll charge it to the room. As they get up, with her leaving her chair out while he pushes his back in, she grabs his arm. He is forced to hold her gaze.

'Rex, I don't understand you. Don't you want to achieve immortality through your photos?'

'No,' says Rex.

'Most people want immortality through ... through their children,' she ventures.

Rex can say nothing. He decided a long time ago to end his 'line'. He throws a serviette he's been scrunching into the chips bowl.

They stare at each other, he into her green/brown eyes, she into his blue wells. The crows and currawongs descend on their vacated table, squawking, gabbling. He wishes he could ask her to reconsider the offer, give back the money her new employers have advanced. He'll get a job to help repay the bit he's spent. He'll even go back to making coffee, if he has to.

Because this is his pressing concern: their own

government dropped Kerrie and Malcolm's research. So what possible interest could a private company have in a virus that makes a pest develop an insatiable appetite for its own kind, apart from its clear potential as a bio-weapon? A virus that will even make a herbivore carnivorous? He works his question to his lips.

She lets go of his arm. 'I'm going back to the room and ordering a massage.'

He steps after her but is distracted by a promising shot: through the fish-bone leaves of the palm above, two sea eagles wheeling like paired brackets, the air between them a parenthesis. He unzips his bag and removes his camera, takes out a polariser and screws it onto the lens. But he doesn't now lift his gaze. He's transfixed by the polariser, the polariser she has bought for him to take photos on the holiday her advance has paid for. He hesitates too long and the eagles stop circling and fly off, their prey vanished.

Five days since they emerged from the cellar. He is completely awake, the sun lancing through the leaves. Hungry. He wishes he'd grabbed that last chip before the currawong claimed it as its prize. Even if it was only a 'memory-chip'. He can't muster a snicker at the corniness of his own pun. The sounds of currawong and crow fade out to be replaced by his present avian company: the magpies making their morning calls, their distinctive chortling. There is a shape by the water. He rises, startled, issuing a strange noise of fright. Soldier jumps up next to him.

The shape turns.

Kerrie again.

Swaying, it occurs to him that there might be an advantage to these visits of hers from beyond the grave. Because if Kerrie is a ghost, then perhaps she can impart some knowledge across the void that will be of use to him. Something to help him, help him survive. His heart sinks. What if Kerrie is merely his imagination? She can only tell him what he already knows of the contagion, which isn't much. Rex considers Soldier carefully. Soldier didn't take much notice of Kerrie when Kerrie was alive. It's hard to tell if Soldier notices Kerrie now.

'Kerrie, you have to help me. If boiling the water doesn't neutralise the contagion, then what does?'

She pouts with those red lips, blood in a bloodless face.

'I don't know what's more loopy,' she says. 'The fact I'm talking to you or that you're talking to me.'

He lets out an exhalation of surprise. '*Now* who's trying to be funny?' he asks.

Soldier stares at Rex, her head rolling from port to starboard as in a rough swell. Does she see Kerrie?

'Kerrie, where should I go? The cities? Sit tight? Go to the shore? Does anyone have the vaccine?'

Kerrie steps closer, her delight gone.

'Oh God, Rex, why didn't you try to stop me?'

'I didn't want to know,' he says.

'According to you, that's the lame excuse of meat-eaters. They don't want to know the suffering an animal goes through to get to their plates. Hypocrite.'

It wasn't the first time she'd called him that. For a vegetarian, he'd consumed three times the average intake of meat through his dogs. He couldn't justify it except to say that he'd inherited Buzz, Roger and Soldier from others. And once they were in this world, he couldn't take them out of it. Even if that meant other animals were ... Yes, he was a hypocrite.

'What can I do, Kerrie?'

'You should have tried to stop me, Rex. Oh God, why didn't you try to stop me?'

She falls to her feet, head between knees, arms wrapped around her legs, and wails the way she did in the cellar.

'I didn't want to know,' he moans. 'I didn't want to know.'

Rex opens his eyes. Was he really awake before? All he sees now is a bright, dappled blur. But he can feel, smell and hear Soldier pawing at him for the umpteenth time. Giving up, she pads over to the creek; puts her nose in the rocks; sniffs around. Focused now, Rex watches her dig up something and eat it. Good. She spits it out. He rolls onto his other side.

'Oh God.'

It's all he can say. He'd never before called on God so often. Or is he now just using the word as an exclamation? Or, in his anger, an expletive? He closes his eyes, but that only shuts out visual distractions from his hunger. And of course his thirst for a drink other than tomato juice. He opens them again.

'Soldier.'

With a rustle, she emerges from the bracken, silver sparkling on its blackened fronds, and pauses, ears tented. He calls again. Rushing over, she whines, cries, licks his face.

'Soldier.'

Her tails wags so hard and her bum wiggles so much, that she almost falls over. She needs him. He gets up, painfully and slowly. He's made his decision.

Soldier will be lost without him, as he would be without her. He was aiming to make her self-sufficient, but now he wants to kill them both. He has tried to imagine coming up behind her and bludgeoning her crown but the image almost made him sick. He must shoot her first, then himself. There is only one nearby place he can think of where he might find either a loaded gun or ammunition for the Colt Python he's got: the military compound. He hopes they are all dead because, if they're not, he knows what he'll try to do.

'Come on, girl,' he says, and Soldier follows, glad to have him back.

At least for a little while.

Rex camouflages the truck with broken branches. Soldier grabs at their ends, ripping off leaves. More hungry than playful, her heart isn't in it. He hauls his supplies back up the slope, along with as many tins as he can manage. He nearly slips once or twice, holding onto the merest tufts of grass or scraggly bushes that hardly claim tenure themselves.

The car's still there. Turning it on, he finds that it has its remaining supply of fuel: a quarter of a tank. No one's been past. No one who's stopped anyway. Besides, he would have heard, even in his delirium. This used to be a busy road. For road trains. Not now. He gets out. Soldier, who was already beside him, shifts to his seat, evidently disappointed.

So that he'll find the spot again, and his remaining cache of tinned tomatoes, he fixes two pieces of wood in a cross formation, picks a bunch of wild, dead flowers and strings the combination to the blackened butt of a tree. A fake roadside memorial.

Swaying in front of the tree, exhausted, he's not sure why he's gone to the effort. If he finds a loaded gun or bullets, he'll make short use of them. And if he doesn't, what would he be coming back to? A dwindling supply of tinned tomatoes, a red-dyed death? He hee-haws drily. At least there will be flowers to mark the spot.

He reopens the driver's door. Soldier quickly bundles across to the front passenger seat before he sits down. As he pulls onto the road, he glimpses

Kerrie in the rear-view mirror, standing in the middle of the road.

Why didn't he try to stop her?

She doesn't wave. He concentrates on the road ahead. He's driven along it many times. He thinks back to when he was still learning its shape.

It's a week after they arrived. He has the windows down as usual when not with Kerrie, the wind blow-drying his hair after his quick morning shower. The destination: nowhere but where there might be 'shots'. Roger is directly behind, in his usual spot, long snout out the window but, timidly, not too far. Buzz hogs the middle, hind legs on the back seat, front paws on the storage compartment behind the handbrake. The sides of the front seats are matted with her gold, white and black hairs. As always, she is trying to edge further forward to claim the front passenger seat, Rex forced to elbow her now and then, in a gentle fashion.

To his left, in an endless stretch of paddock, dry and pitiless, Rex catches sight of something amazing. He stops the car and backs up to it, watching the last of the yellow-throated miners flying from its innards.

A bale of barbed wire, lying on the ground, rusted to an approximation of a giant's bird nest. The scale of it makes the grown honeyeaters which flew out of it appear to be chicks.

Rex takes out his zoom, hoping the birds will

reclaim their readymade nest then, at the right moment, he can beep the horn and capture them erupting. Recapture the magic digitally.

Buzz and Roger paddle the backseat restlessly; stopping the car generally means they're getting out.

Rex's eye is distracted by more movement.

A dog, blue and black, flecked with white. The white of age? Rex reassesses. No, a blue-heeler kelpie-cross, half-hiding behind the spinifex grass; youngish. He removes Buzz's collar and grabs a lead, then gets out, leaving his irate dogs in the car so they won't scare it off. Checking the fence for ceramic insulators – the sign it may be electrified – and finding none, he hops over carelessly, getting a closer view. Compact with a wide triangle mouth, a bit like a crocodile's, her teats are hanging low – she must have recently borne a litter. She backs away. He approaches more slowly, trying to coax her with cooing, Buzz and Roger's barking not helping.

She slinks forward on her belly. Rex reaches out and holds his palm open for her to sniff, then, passing inspection, pats her gently. With a quick sleight of hand, he slips the collar over her head.

Returning to the car, Buzz fogs up the window with her barking. He tells her sharply to back off; Roger, in placidity, merely wags his tail. Rex pushes the dog in, tail between its legs. She tries climbing to be next to the back seat window. Getting away from the other two?

Rex gets in. Buzz growls, sparking growling in the new dog. Rex calls Buzz in the front, Buzz only hesitating for a second, before grinning.

Driving home, the blue heeler sits up the back, Roger leaning against the seat, their wet noses touching. Buzz beside Rex, beaming smugly; she's finally got the front seat.

Pulling up at the house, Kerrie is unimpressed. He hammers a stake into their lawn then connects a chain from it to Buzz's collar around the blue heeler's neck. *The same chain that would later tether Kerrie …*

The dog fights when he washes her, Buzz and Roger slinking away under the veranda, hoping it isn't their turn next. For such a small, compact dog, she's tough and it's a struggle. He rinses the soapy water out of her coat with a watering can and the lawn is doused black. He lets her go and she flicks her head although he was sure he'd kept the water out of her ears.

It proves a similar struggle getting her over the threshold. This is his first real inkling that she might be a traditional, outside farm dog. In hindsight, her trying to climb up the back seat to the window might mean she's used to riding in the tray of a ute. The shaking-the-head routine could mean she isn't used to a collar, either.

That night, she moans and whimpers on the matt next to their bed. He pulls her up and cuddles her, and eventually she settles.

'This means we're keeping her,' says Kerrie over his shoulder, less a question than a resigned statement.

He stops in the roadhouse for breakfast the next morning, with the new dog tied up outside. (Buzz and Roger were mortified when he left without them.) Eyeing the steamed glass of the bain-marie, he orders what appears safest.

'No bacon? You don't want bacon?' asks the pinched-faced woman in her curiously old-fashioned print frock.

'No.'

'Sausages?'

'No thanks.'

Her face tightens in disapproval; a red fist. She probably thinks he's being cheap.

He sits on what was once a white plastic chair next to what was once a white plastic table, both grubby now, to face his meal of brackish coffee and snotty eggs, wishing he hadn't asked for sunny side up.

When the woman comes back with the hottest sauce she can find, American mustard, he inquires about the dog.

She takes a quick peek through the flyscreen.

'Nah, I dunno. Um, nah, dunno. Maybe ask Gus.'

She hobbles back to the counter, revealing a man sitting in the corner under a dartboard. The man shoots up and shuffles over in a dance, one arm forward. Rex leans back, instinctively.

'Gus.'

A square face of red planes with a triangular nose. White, curled hair against a red forehead. Green and red eyes. Skin, sand-papered red. Red.

Rex takes Gus' coarse hand before Gus makes a long assessment of the dog. He sits down, plastic scraping the polished concrete floor. Nodding his head, he tells Rex he knows the guy who owns her. The guy won't be back for another twelve months.

'Do you think I should try to get in touch with him?' Rex asks.

'When he worked out she wasn't on the back of his fuckin' ute, he didn't fuckin' do a U-ie, did he? He's a mad bastard, the way he drives. All I'll say, it was a fuckin' good thing he didn't have her tied up.'

Gus says the dog's name is Soldier. Rex's lip curls. He doesn't like the military name. He hasn't got to name any of his dogs. He briefly considers calling her something else.

'You're not much of a vegetarian, are ya?'

'How did you – ?'

'Come on, we're not fuckin' stupid in the bush. You've got two dogs already. Three now with this one. What do you propose feeding 'em? Grass?'

'No.'

'What's your fuckin' problem with eating meat anyway?'

Rex doesn't feel like this conversation, but Gus has

him pinned with that red nose.

'It's the way we treat them,' he begins slowly, then reluctantly discovers momentum. 'Poor things, penned up in small cages from birth, only to be cruelly and violently slaughtered in abattoirs.'

To his surprise, Gus agrees.

'But not *my* sheep and cows. They have, you know, "free range". They're "organic", too. I don't mince up cows to feed to my cows – none of that shit. Mad cow disease, swine flu – that's how you get shit like that. They're not fuckin' cannibals. And when it comes time to kill 'em, I do it myself. In an abattoir, they know what's going to happen, don't they? Those places stink of fear. But I lead 'em off on their own, cut their throats before they fuckin' know it.'

Rex blinks. 'Perhaps I could buy my meat from you?'

Gus leans back in the plastic chair. With a squeak, its legs readjust on the concrete floor. 'Of course free-range and organic costs extra.'

'I'm willing to pay.'

The fence whizzes past on his right, endless fence. Rex realises he's gripping the wheel. He tries to relax his cramping fingers but can't.

Of course he was willing to pay. It wasn't his money. It was Kerrie's.

Is that why he didn't really try to stop her?

Oh God, what has he done? What has he *not*

done? It's the end of the world. No, the end of *their* world. *Their* world? What is he thinking! *Our* world, our world, humans. He thinks of the music he loved, the photos, the art. The things you can like about us. What has he done? What has he *not* done?

Soldier pants next to him.

The entrance to the military compound looms. Pressing the brake, the car skids to a halt, the dust flouncing like the trail of a bridal gown. Soldier falls on the floor. He staggers out, Soldier plopping out a moment later; he's beaten her for once. The guard station appears empty, the door ajar. There's a black mound on the road like a rolled-up carpet. He ignores it and makes for the gate. His fingers reach through the wires, grip then shake, a chain and padlock preventing it from opening more than the tiniest arc. He looks up: the gate must be nearly three metres high, in height with the fence. Topped with razor wire, too. Even if he had the strength to climb and didn't cut himself to pieces in the process, that would leave him on foot. He can't see any buildings behind the fence all the way to the horizon. It could be a hundred kilometres to the compound and any weapons. Besides, he won't leave Soldier.

'Oh God.'

He turns, falling against the wire, slipping down it as it jolts against his back. Soldier's sniffing that dark shape on the road. Calling her, she waddles over. He reaches for the ruff of her neck he likes to sink his fingers into. She falls in his lap. The sun, the stinking hot sun. He can't take much more of this.

He squints into the brightness. Where's Kerrie now? She thought she was an environmentalist. He laughs. In a way she was, eradicating the greatest pest of all.

Thirst, hunger, thirst. He's got to get bullets, he's got to end these thoughts, these cravings, end this life that's short anyway – end it even faster. He suddenly moves, Soldier jumping backwards, a hairy crayfish. He pulls himself up the gate, totters to the car. Soldier, cautious, jumps through the door and into the back. Rex slides gingerly into the car, turns it on; the petrol nearly in the red. He's only ever driven up this side of the military fence, the side that spans the length to town. It veers off at a right-angle at that point. He's never driven up that side. How long *is* that side? Is there another entrance? Will it be locked too? He hasn't thought this through. He hasn't thought anything through.

His heart is pumping wildly. His aching, breaking heart. Poor Soldier will be left more alone than him.

He takes off, veering round that shape – a dead wombat, he can see clearly now – and gets up speed, scanning the fence for holes he has no hope will be there.

'Rex, you don't say anything.'

He hits the steering wheel in frustration. There must be a way in, there must.

'Rex?'

A drain under the fence … something.

'Rex?'

'Yes!'

Kerrie has reclaimed her seat next to him.

'Rex, do you know what it's like just getting monosyllabic answers for your efforts while you're scoping for possible shots?'

He isn't. This time he isn't. His camera is the furthest thing from his mind. Well, he *is* hunting for shots in a way. One for Soldier, one for himself. He didn't know Kerrie was talking to him.

'You can't even answer me now,' she says, exasperated.

'I've nothing left to say,' he returns quickly.

Kerrie loosens her seatbelt. This maddens him. Why's she wearing a seatbelt? She's dead!

'But *I* do, Rex, *I* do. I'm with someone who isn't there half the time.'

He forces himself not to scan the fence in case she can accuse him of framing shots. He realises he's taking too long to answer. This makes him snap.

'*You* left *me*, Kerrie. Left me to cope with this on my own. And not only that: you left me in a way that almost killed me as well.'

Kerrie gulps back a sob. 'I don't understand. It should be over for you now.'

He snarls. 'Yes, but it might not be over for Soldier.'

He turns to where Soldier is cowering in the back. He orders her to jump in the front. She complies, taking her spot.

An old Kombi van ahead, adorned in hippy swirls.

He stops, wheezing with anxiety. Tapping on the tank with a spanner, it resounds hollowly. Before peering in a side window, he takes in the lay of the land. A few corpses in the ditch along the side of the road. He forces his eyes back to the van but his thoughts are still in that ditch with them. He opens the sliding door. Just useless items left. One of those bodies looked small … He lifts the front bonnet. Tiny … Everything worth taking in the engine has also gone. He shuts it with a start, having seen something through the front windshield: two toddler shoes hanging from the rear-view mirror.

Back on the road, another vehicle ahead, a ute. By the dint on its roof, it must have rolled. This time when he stops he doesn't turn off the engine. When he started the car last time, it spluttered.

Similar story. Nothing essential left. Someone's been rummaging along here, pretty thoroughly. Opening his car door, his hand slips on the catch. Sweating. Stretching his now-grey shirt and wiping it with the other hand, he sees that they're both shaking.

On the move again. The fuel needle on empty, but the red light hasn't turned on yet.

'Oh God, Oh God.'

This is where he'll die, out on this lifeless road. This is where.

Soldier is curled up.

Something different up ahead this time: sheep. A herd grazing along the stretch of land between the road and the fences. He slows down. Soldier unfurls. Their long faces stare at him with dim recollection – a human – as he drives through. Several shuffle in front of the car.

'Come on, come on!'

He beeps furiously, the sound almost an affront in the reclaimed 'silence'. Their backs make woollen waves. He didn't want to slow down again. Every time he speeds up, that's more petrol. Soldier yaps and wags her tail and the sheep part more swiftly. He finds a wink for her. Yep, a farm dog, for sure.

He passes a windmill, slowly spinning in the wind. Its shadow churns the buttery grass.

Something doesn't add up about that wombat.

Flashing past, to his left: an honesty box with a sign advertising horse manure for a dollar a kilo, the white plastic bags still full and upright, but no doubt already hard and desiccated.

Wombats are nocturnal, as far as he knows. What was it doing out in the day? Well, who's to say it didn't die at night?

Up ahead, to the left, two tractor tyres half-buried and sloppily painted white, positioned side by side as 'posh' entrance arches to a property. Now adjacent to it, he catches a glimpse of the long driveway lined with heat-stressed pines, the front gate flat on the ground. Two brindled mares and a colt stand in the shade, tails swishing.

Should he check the estate for a gun or, at the least, bolt cutters? No. The thorough way this stretch of road has been picked over, it's unlikely any houses fronting it will be left un-frisked.

The wombat.

Why do his thoughts keep returning to that poor wombat?

No, the road; he must concentrate on the road instead; on his driving and scanning the fence. But the road, there's also something unusual about the road? Something ... missing – something, that is, apart from the absence of moving cars.

A flash of brown. He swerves. Soldier nearly falls out the window. He brakes, leaving smelly rubber ticks on the baking bitumen. The kangaroo, a giant brown flea, hops, uninjured, into the acacia bushes.

He glances away from the road. The comb-over tufts of grass lift in the wind.

His heart pounds. Soldier jumps in the back seat.

That's what's missing!

Road-kill, the absence of fresh road-kill! Now that he thinks about it, ever since emerging from the cellar he's only seen the dried, mummified bits of animal that must be left over from when the contagion first hit, now starting to peel and flake off the tar like posters.

Excepting, of course, that wombat. That wombat was a fresh kill …

He does a U-turn. He hopes he has enough petrol to make it back to the gate.

The blood on the wombat is dry but freshly dried. No expert at forensics, he ventures a guess that its death can't be more than twelve hours old.

He examines the gate more closely. The levers have been sawn through on closer inspection. Of course! The gates would have been electronically operated. That source of power must be gone by now, even for the military. That's why the chain and padlock to secure it instead – they've destabilised the opening mechanism. He should have brought his bolt cutters. That's assuming they were left in his shed. Or rummaged for some in that estate. He can ram the gate. Peering closer at the lock, he can see that won't work either; the lock and chain are made of high-tensile steel. His panic pings back and forth in his stomach, a game of squash. He's going to die anyway. Turning to the car, he wonders if he should turn back for the tinned tomatoes. Stumbling forward, he stops. Why? Even if he makes it, he won't leave that creek bed/deathbed again. He won't be able to walk back. And he'll be even weaker from more days on tinned tomatoes, not stronger. He hasn't thought this through. He hasn't thought anything through …

Wait! He swivels back to the gate. Whoever ran that wombat down must be coming back … they wouldn't bother locking the gate otherwise. Then again, they might be inside already?

Where's Soldier?

He turns to see her sniffing the wombat. He goes to the car, grabs his sword, returns to its black barrel shape. He raises the sword above his head, feeling dizzyingly sick, and brings it down.

'Help me.'

He lifts the sword, catching an eyeful of disorienting sunlight, and again lets the sword fall. This time the leg separates. He kicks it at Soldier. She scans dumbly from it to him.

'Bloody hell, Soldier!'

Now she looks mortified. But she must be starving, starving to death like him. He falls back against the car. Sliding to the ground, the car shielding him from the afternoon sun, the sun a medusa. Only, instead of turning everything to stone – ash.

Three hours later. The sun has nearly set. A blood-mopped sky. Rex has parked off the road, behind a thick stand of scrub, to the left of the gate. With a smouldering stick, he flicks the leg of the wombat from the fire he's made. It rolls along the ground, crumbed in twigs and leaves. Soldier sniffs it. He thinks about covering the coals with dirt and lying on that for the night. He remembers from TV, or reading it somewhere, that that's what the Aborigines used to do.

He sets about the task. With the last ember buried, a thousand eyes slowly wink open above: stars. In their brilliant light, Rex lays out his blankets. The leg having cooled, Soldier takes first a tentative, then a more appreciative, bite. Soon she is devouring it with relish, holding it with her neat paws. His heart contracts at the image. He's glad she's survived. Otherwise he'd be totally alone in this. Perhaps it's selfish to be glad she's with him, rather than perishing with Buzz and Roger. He opens a tin of tomatoes. He used to like tomatoes but not for every meal, his ongoing 'last meal'. He retches, struggling not to throw up, and lies down, sickly and faint. Without even a pillow for his head, he rolls up a jacket for a semblance of comfort. It occurs to him he's lost track of what day it is. Before he knows it, darkness washes over him.

It is a fortnight after he found Soldier. He is with Kerrie at the weir. The lake has been dry so long the dead trees and fences from before it was flooded are visible again, caked in dry mud. In the shallowest spots, where water still pools briefly, one or two bushes have actually sprouted. The lakebed is cracked like a bowl smashed into a million pieces, each piece a shallow ceramic dish of its own.

He and Kerrie lay out their blankets and picnic things up the bank, eat, drink and make love. She rolls away, lifting her legs in the air before leaning them on the creamy bole of a tree. Pretending to stretch or are other motives at play? He wonders idly if she has stopped taking the pill.

He heads down the bank. The dirt dishes would make a good shot. With Kerrie's money, he's bought a tilt-shift lens. With that, he can make them seem like a surreal dinner party. But they weren't allowed camera or dogs on this picnic. It was going to be 'romantic'. And, if he was lucky, 'sexy'.

He can come back.

He locates the sun. The light's perfect *now*. He scopes Kerrie, still on her back and with white legs blended into the white of the trunk. Did she want to make passionate love to him or simply conceive? For the first time in ages, she'd been the one pushing for sex. He feels tricked, *used*.

Tilting her head back, she asks if he's sent off his latest photos to publications.

He walks to her through the grass, its hollow reediness like organ pipes. 'Yes, they're not interested. Don't worry,' he adds, *'you're* going to make your impact on the world.'

She reaches for her straw hat beside her. He continues, unchecked.

'But there should also be prizes for the people who go unnoticed, don't you think? Who have the least impact on the world, the complete unknowns. The ones who *don't* leave a mark should also be celebrated … except … No, wait! That would negate their achievement.'

He laughs; she doesn't. He briefly feels contrite, but it isn't deep or lasting.

'Can't you be proud of me, Kerrie? I'm proud of you.'

Kerrie puts her hat over her face to shade her eyes.

'No, you're not.'

They pull up in their driveway, greeted by yapping dogs. Opening the car door, they surround Rex; Soldier muscling her way through, fighting for her new stake in his attentions. They whine, bark, jump up. Bending down, Rex tries to make a fuss of them equally. Kerrie comes round the car and joins them.

'Remember that dream I told you about?' she asks, her face ghostly, even then.

Rex takes his eyes off the dogs for a second. Roger lands a smooch on his cheek.

'Which one?' he asks, wiping the slobber from his face; Kerrie has many dreams.

'You were asked: "If you were stranded on a deserted island for the rest of your life and you could only take three things, what would they be?" And you replied, "My dogs, all three of them."'

Rex rises to his feet, his dogs using him as a

stretching pole. He knew where this was going. 'Did I now?' he tries to say lightly.

'Only you didn't think it through. In eight years they were all dead, because dogs have a shorter lifespan, and yet you still had at least thirty years to go.'

Buzz retrieves her deflated basketball and knocks it against his knee. He takes the ball. Buzz doesn't let go.

'Stupid,' he jokes.

'Yes,' says Kerrie.

Rex lets go of the ball. Soldier grabs the free half and she and Buzz play tug-of-war as Roger dances madly round them.

Rex and Kerrie walk to house. He doesn't want another fight. Perhaps he can head it off before they go inside, leave their problems on the doormat.

Welcome.

He stops, wiping his feet. 'Kerrie, I like humans too.'

'No, you don't.'

Rex reconsiders. 'No.'

Kerrie makes a gesture as if to say, 'Point proven.'

He winks at her. 'But I make an exception with a chosen few.'

She scans from him to the dogs jostling at his feet, not wanting to be separated from their master at the door. Something flickers behind her eyes and her face screws up in that vulnerability he's now decided isn't so rare after all. 'The dogs always go to you. We were given Buzz together as a pup, but she still goes to you first. Is that what would happen if we had kids?'

He gives up being pleasant. 'If I was the one who solely fed and walked them, then probably.'

Kerrie huffs. 'You don't walk kids.'

He opens the door and is carried inside on a wave of fur.

Kerrie calls after him. 'You even have a dog's name!'

'Rex was Mum's favourite dog,' he says, on auto-pilot now.

Kerrie slams the door from the outside.

Rex wakes with a start. A vivid line of dawn has just opened on the horizon like someone peeping through a trapdoor into a lightless room. He listens. A sound he's not so used to anymore: another vehicle. He peers through the skein of bushes. Two phosphorescent feelers: head lights. Soldier barks. He grabs her muzzle and pulls her close.

'Shhh!'

A black Hummer runs the wombat over for a second time and stops at the fence. Someone gets out of the front passenger seat, dropping into the dirt. Rex nearly gasps until he figures the horns sprouting from his head must be from a cheap plastic Viking helmet. The man's topless; lower half, army greens, and not some kind of desert faun. He fiddles with the lock. About twenty, lean. Or is that emaciated?

Rex tries to call, get up, show himself. Anything.

'Hurry up!' is yelled from the Hummer.

Rex's mouth is so dry his lips catch on his teeth.

The guy undoes the lock on the chain.

Rex could at least show himself.

And swings the heavy gate, grunting.

Rex can't find his feet, either.

The Hummer drives through in a short burst. In a cartoonish display, the horned guy runs after it, getting a face-full of dust. There is wisecracking from within the Hummer at his ghostly makeup.

Rex pushes through the bushes even as they scratch at him. Soldier stays so close at heel she is almost a fur boot.

The dust-covered guy already has the chain looped through the poles –

'Hurry up!'

– coughs, wipes at his eyes with his dusty bare arms, and blinds himself.

'I … just a … ah-choo!'

He can't get anything out for sneezing. Rex pushes aside the last branch that was trying to clothesline him. Soldier breaks away and crouches forward.

A shot.

Rex stops. Soldier scoots back between his legs.

An M16 waving out the window. The man holding it yells, 'Fuckin' forget it.'

The helmeted guy feels his way to the front passenger door. With barely a foot in, the driver takes off, eliciting another round of crowing.

Rex waits for the dust cloud to peter out. Why didn't he show himself? The same initial reluctance in the general store again prevented him from revealing himself. Pushing the gate, he finds that it opens. The chain snakes to the ground, coiling in the puffing dust. He takes the unfastened lock still hooked on the wire of the gate. He'll pick up the chain in a minute. For now, he wants to watch the Hummer to the horizon. It blinks out in a wash of first-coat blackness.

Grabbing the end of the chain, he pulls it in the direction the Hummer disappeared until the chain forms a straight line: an arrow pointing in the direction he'll head in the morning.

Soldier whimpers, by his feet. He desperately hopes their car will start.

The sun streams above the horizon, illuminating a light mist. Rex rolls up his blankets after giving them a shake, then folds his small tarp. The ground of his bed is still warm. Soldier wanders far enough to perform her ablutions but still keep a beady eye on him. His stomach screeches hunger.

Packing the car, he thinks how lucky they were the Hummer's high beams didn't pick out their Cressida behind its meagre camouflage of scribbly bush. After a quick meal of tinned tomato, and Soldier a return to her wombat leg, they get in the car. Holding his breath, Rex turns the ignition. Phew.

The tracks of the Hummer aren't hard to follow; plus, they've driven in a straight line. What's curious is the fact they've gone off-road. He drives fast enough not to get bogged in the silted sand but slow enough not to raise much dust.

The needle is lost below the red of the petrol gauge, out of sight behind charcoal plastic. At any moment the car will stop. Panic constricts his chest. Just how big is this military zone? It could be hundreds of square kilometres – thousands maybe. What's to say he'll find them? He should have announced his presence. The fact that man could waste a bullet on the air in a dramatic flourish, surely means they'd have two to spare.

Rex feels a sudden and unexpected tinge of regret. He's been so adamant about ending his life at the end of a barrel, he couldn't have chosen a more inhospitable, less scenic, spot. A river would have been more pleasant: he could have weighed himself down to sink to the tilled sand at the bottom, lodged himself under the complicated plumbing of tree roots, like a suiciding croc. But that leaves Soldier. She was hard enough to wash; drowning her would be nigh impossible. At least she'd have had water if he'd left her on the bank.

Idiot, idiot! He slaps the steering wheel. Out here, she'll die of thirst, just like him. He gazes across at her wide, yawning mouth and slippery-dip tongue with its kick at the end; the broadest smile he's ever been given.

'I'm sorry, Soldier, I'm sorry.'

She licks her chops. He hits a furrow and the car bounces. Righting the wheel, he glimpses a collection of white structures half a kilometre up ahead, shining like silver spaceships on the moon, and just as lonely. Parked next to them, the Hummer.

Yes, yes, he's found them!

'We'll be okay, Soldier, we'll be okay.'

Soldier's mouth shuts with a slap. Rex's own jaw sets, the corners of his mouth straightening. Still something is stopping him from driving straight up to their camp. There is a mound to the east. He veers towards that instead, inching forward slowly so as not to kick up dust and betray their position prematurely. Why this cautiousness, why? This belligerent mania to control the manner of his own death, the timing? Does he still hold out hope?

The engine sputters and dies at the first incline, but safely out of sight of the camp. Rex collects dead branches, Soldier panting beside him, then lays them like fans over his car as camouflage.

The mound is like a half-buried giant golf ball with the top sliced off at an angle. The top is bare jutting stone, red and blue. The sides support coarse bush. He and Soldier amble up, Rex weighed down with camera bag.

Behind a tanker-shaped rock on the highest point, he swaps the mount on his camera from a prime to a telephoto lens. Then sets up his tripod. About to take the lens cap off, he hesitates, remembering a scene in *Indiana Jones and the Last Crusade*. Holding his camera facedown to the ground instead, only then does he remove the lens cap. Keeping his hand a few centimetres from the lens, he then points it in the direction of the military. Waving his hand in front of the camera, his palm doesn't appear to catch a circle of light. He then glances round, feeling foolish; the sun is behind him. This isn't a game. He squints through the eyepiece at the campsite.

Only one guy, with glasses. Unimaginatively, Rex names him IQ. It takes till sundown for IQ's mates to emerge, which makes sense. Like vampires, they've been forced to sleep in the day, out of the insufferable sun, to rise in the cool of night.

Including IQ – the lookout – they number five altogether. The Viking in his Viking helmet he christens Thor. The man who fired the M16, black and muscular, he christens Tank, taking inspiration from the rock he's leaning on. There is an older, darker skinned guy with a brilliantly white beard, sitting down on a black metal case. His inspiration failing him, he simply calls him Boss. A skinny red head, unmercifully burnt in the sun, is Ross, after a guy Rex once knew. Only Boss still wears his full desert camouflage. The others have mixed military with civilian clothes to varying extent.

A blanket of shadow is slowly pulled up the long stretch of desert as the sun sinks, tucking this part of the world in for the night. Out here where the sky forms half of every view.

Flies hum at his mouth. One docks in his nose. Snorting and spitting, Rex decides that if the military that helped foster the virus is fucked, then everyone is.

'Why aren't they in their buildings?' he asks Soldier. 'They're pretty exposed there. It doesn't make sense.'

He glimpses a concrete water tank amid their tarps and tents. Reappraising the view, he decides Boss and Co. aren't merely resting; they're guarding this zealously. That's maybe why they're camped out here, to be next to the tank. Seems like they've blocked the pipes in case it rains and their supply's contaminated. Would they spare him any? Unlikely.

Do they have hope? Are they expecting rescue? Is this all that's left of them? Are they postponing the inevitable until their last reserves of water have gone?

'What do you think, Soldier?'

Soldier doesn't answer.

'Soldier?'

He turns, edging backwards down the slope.

'Soldier ...?'

He pushes through the spinifex, stumbling upon a

shallow gully hitherto hidden from his site by shrub. Pushing his way through charred branches, he spies bits of twisted metal, human arms, legs ...

'*Soldier ...?*'

Leaning forward at a tangle of black, as if to drink from a creek, she turns, smiling.

'What is it, girl?'

The black isn't water; it's a pit. Lunging for his dog and missing her, he falls.

Above, a rent opening onto the cobalt sky, Soldier barking down at him.

'Shush, Soldier, shush!'

Her busy mouth snaps shut. Rex quickly pats himself down. He's bruised but nothing's broken. He knows what broken bones feel like. He sits up gingerly. Glancing round, he sees he's in a corridor, underground. He gazes up again. The roof's been blasted off.

It is a month after he and Kerrie went to the weir. Night time. They are sitting in the lounge, TV off, snuggled together on the couch, Buzz, Roger and Soldier all in their various 'spots.' It's Kerrie's birthday, the third of her birthdays they have shared together. She has been hinting for weeks she deserves a present that justifies her patronage.

She finishes leafing through the photo album. To his surprise, she has tears in her eyes.

'They're beautiful … Savage, too. Those tiny birds flying out of that giant nest on the ground – surreal. How did you get *that*? You have an amazing eye. My last year is all here. Buzz, Roger's and Soldier's, too. But …'

But? He's sure she didn't say this at the time. He waits for her to continue.

'But, Rex …'

'Yes?'

'*You're* not there.'

He thinks about this. He owns a tripod, his camera has a self-timer. He uses them for long-exposure shots or in low-light. And yet he never uses them to put himself in the picture. Why?

For the first time he considers the question Kerrie asks of herself all the time: If I died now, what record would be left of me? His sudden expression shocks Kerrie into wiping her eyes and forcing a smile.

'Sorry, it's beautiful, darling. I mean, they're beautiful. It's a beautiful gift.'

Rex looks away from the sun and Soldier and into the darkness of the corridor. The answer catches him with the force of a blow. He now knows why he didn't try to stop Kerrie's work.

He wanted this to happen.

CHAPTER THREE

Rex puts the book on the marble-top table. His father sees its title and winces.

'Rex.'

'What?'

'*A History Of Torture*?'

Rex says nothing; his father lights a cigarette.

'Last week it was *The Animal Holocaust*.'

Rex smirks. 'I like to know my enemy.'

His father takes a swig of his can of whisky and dry. 'I feel sorry for the young'uns 'cause they feel sorry for themselves. You're the privileged unhappy. We humans have also done some great things.'

Rex wonders what time this recollection dates from. He eyeballs his surrounds more carefully. He is in the courtyard at the back of the café. It's in shadow and his father's having a drink which means the working day's over. About 5:00pm. Looking down,

Rex sees that he is wearing a brown apron that hangs down to his knees, stained in places a darker brown from coffee. Scrutinising his hands, it is like they have been inked for prints, but a brown ink instead of the standard blue. He can now place this memory more precisely. He isn't visiting the café; he still works there. Before the time of Kerrie. They were long, hard, dull, days but were they also rewarding?

He takes this opportunity to ask a question he didn't at the time.

'Dad, what was Mum like?'

His father gasps, his mouth moving like an earthed fish. He puts down his can, sloshing with the bit he leaves to ash into. The question is out of character for Rex. Eventually his father says shortly: 'Your mother was lucky. She died in perfection.'

Without thinking, he downs the last of his whisky before leaning towards Rex, spluttering. 'But *you're* not going to die like that.'

Abruptly, he tries to mend his words. 'I mean …'

Rex knows what he means: his father doesn't want Rex to die early. But his father's unintended meaning is more apt: No, Rex *won't* die in perfection.

Morning. A week since he and Kerrie opened the trapdoor of their cellar. A week, and he has found another darkness. Lighting a taper, Rex and Soldier have traced out three hundred metres of concrete corridor, terminating at a solid iron door he can't open and beginning where the blast has brought down the ceiling. (He'd helped Soldier join him by piling up the copious furniture into something of a staircase. Why all the furniture should have been in that section, Rex could only guess.)

He's rationed out all the food he's found in parcels dotted along the corridor, one each a day. The appropriate volume of blessed bottled water as well. And something very special, a Merlot. He's also found guns, plenty of guns. In truth, he should have shot himself and Soldier by now.

Best of all, he's come upon two bullets for his Colt Python, now loaded and stored in the glovebox of the car – the car, which he's filled up with petrol he's also found.

He's stopped carrying the sword everywhere with him but has found a combat knife he keeps tucked in his trousers.

Days pass in which he avoids thoughts of Kerrie, the kid. He composes a song which he infinitely improvises.

The friendships that I battered,
The friendships that I flattered.
The days that I have strengthened,
The days that I have lengthened.
The dreams I never willed.
The people I have …

He feels his strength returning. He knows this is a short reprieve, that he'll die anyway, but he is enjoying the stay of execution.

The corridor is almost becoming homey. He's set up a bed for himself and Soldier. The smell is the worst bit. He hasn't had the strength to haul the body pieces out yet. He'll start tomorrow. The first job, after eating and drinking, was rigging up something to hide the entrance.

It's very lucky those militia didn't see the blast, or discover the corridor. Very lucky. For him of course.

The fact they seem to be waiting around to die would indicate they don't have much hope of long-term survival either.

The people that I've missed,
All proof that I exist?

His first long draught of water after the month of alcohol and soft drinks in the cellar, and the tinned tomatoes of the last week was a pleasure of such leering intensity. He felt like a desiccated sponge expanding to a bloated happiness. Funny how the simplest thing in life, the largest component of life in fact, should finally rear up to claim its place as also the most important.

He's separated from the pile of furniture a couple of chairs, a table, and set them up in what must have once been an industrial kitchen. He's brought in the sunlight through an overhead vent, illuminating his chair in a spotlight. The unchained interrogation prisoner. He and Soldier eat a lunch of beef jerky together, Rex's vegetarianism necessarily consigned to the past. His metal fork clinks on tin plate, Soldier's slopping on the floor – she always drags her meal from her bowl.

Rex regards her humorously. 'Kerrie doesn't look like she's joining us.'

How Kerrie would hate his new domestic arrangements.

Moving to the outback with Kerrie's new job, Rex missed a lot about Melbourne. He missed his few friends, the ones who found his coldness neither discomforting nor a challenge. He missed working on his car with his dad. Not the Cressida, but the 165 T-bird Ford his father had bought for him and was helping him fix up. Not that they got much time to.

His father was a mechanic before he owned the café. He'd told Rex his ideal café one drunken afternoon after work, when Rex was still in his father's employ. Like his tastes in cars, his father's tastes in cafés also leant towards Americana. He wanted to buy – not pay rent to a mongrel – but buy a disused petrol station, preferably an old one, and fix it up as a café. Play fifties and sixties music and get waiters and waitresses to take out food on roller skates, *not* rollerblades.

Might have worked. If he'd ever won the lottery.

The fact his father never achieved his dream was something else Rex hated about the world. Beholding Soldier in the dimness, a poor mutt dumped on the side of the road, he realises he has a list of similar complaints stretching interminable.

I don't know why she swallowed the fly.
Perhaps we'll die.

He wanted this to happen.

Sunset. He goes outside to the top of the giant golf ball. There they are, the same five. They don't seem to have gone anywhere since he arrived. Is there nothing left to ransack within close proximity? Do they have petrol? They seem to use the scant wood to heat things up. He's found petrol which he uses to light small fires. He's also refilled the tank in his car, and the jerry cans in the boot. And he's filled the boot with tinned food.

Should he tell them about his stash? He's calculated he has three months on his own. With the seven of them, they'd have two weeks.

No. They're all going to die anyway.

He wants to be the last.

Scrambling down the escarpment with Soldier, he spots a goanna: a grease Golem with tuning fork tongue. It moves in staccato as if seen through the flashing black/white of disco lights. Soldier stares transfixed. It tastes them on the air and lumbers mechanically between the rocks. Soldier lurches forward but Rex calls her back. He should really encourage her but can't. When you see a tree, you're only seeing half of it, an iceberg a tenth, a man a millionth, yet an animal: purpose. But a domestic animal, like Soldier, is closed in the same defeat as its master.

He and Soldier climb down into the corridor.

He sets out candles. He wishes he could set a place for Soldier until he remembers how she eats. Focusing on the empty spot across from him, he tries an experiment, getting up and laying out an extra place. Sitting down, he discovers it's worked.

'You want to haunt this land forever?'

'Something like that,' he says to Kerrie.

He's been wondering when she'd turn up again. He pours himself the prized wine. Should he waste any on her? Out of civility, he doles out a glass. Drinking his greedily, he immediately feels intoxicated. She is wearing her fetching red dress with a white linen flower sewn to the base of the left shoulder strap.

There is a knock at the door.

Confused, Rex grabs his M16 and jumps to his feet, Soldier rising with him.

'It's okay,' says Kerrie. 'It's just Malcolm. I invited him over, remember.'

She walks to the door. It's the front door to their outback house.

'Ah, Kerrie, *sans* shoes, *avec* hat.'

Malcolm has come for dinner. Rex has floated back to a few weeks after he gave Kerrie the photo album.

Malcolm is alone. Gary couldn't come – according to Malcolm, he's on the verge of tapping into the multiverse.

'What I'm about, is teaching the girls to think,' says Malcolm, planting a wet kiss on Kerrie's cheek before shoving warm Champagne in Rex's hand.

Rex guesses that Malcolm's referring to their research assistants. Malcolm sits at the head of the table.

'Oh, you mind?'

Rex says nothing and Kerrie titters. Malcolm picks up a conversation he and Kerrie must have begun at work.

'The best thing for the Americans now, economically-speaking, would be to colonise another country. Preferably one without an indigenous population or, at the very least, a meek one. Those Arabs are such intransigents.'

Kerrie dips her fingers in the wax to make rose petals on the burgundy placemat.

She indicates Rex with a nod. 'Malcolm, we shouldn't talk about work. For two reasons.'

Malcolm leans towards Kerrie. 'Did you see my photo in what counts for a paper in this precinct?'

Kerrie laughs. 'Was it an identikit photo?'

Malcolm leans back, pushing his furious curl of grey away from his left eyebrow. 'I don't write the news but I can choose if I make it. This was about my winning at the club.'

'Slumming it?' asks Kerrie.

Remembering it now, Rex ponders for the first time what Kerrie liked in Malcolm. His sense of humour, albeit a twisted one? Was Rex ever anything less than grim?

'So what are *your* hobbies, Rex?' asks Malcolm in his perpetually amused tone.

'Dogs, cars and photography,' says Kerrie, filling in Rex's blank. He'd promised to behave.

'How refreshingly simple. Honest. My hobbies. Number one: "nerding". Well, nerding would have to rank very high. Yes, it *is* a verb, thank you. Talking of nerding, Kerrie, did you get a chance to watch that *Hades* series I downloaded?'

'I get home about the same time you do,' protests Kerrie.

'You call this dustbowl home?' he laughs.

Malcolm turns to Rex. '*You'd* have time to watch them, not working.'

'Rex *is* working,' says Kerrie quickly.

'Oh, yes, the great *artiste*. In your spare time, I meant. You do know what I'm talking about? *Hades* – only the best TV series since the last?'

Rex doesn't watch drama, only docos. He nods anyway.

'Geek kudos to you. Let's see, what else do I love? Freshly baked bread. Quilting. Kisses in the rain. It's patently obvious. Oh, Kerrie, did you see that field marshal that flew in yesterday? She's officially my hot slut of the week. She has a boyfriend back home – vague nuisance – but I'm going to bed her. Bet on it?'

He puts forward a hand, which Rex wants to slap away. Kerrie takes it.

'Excuse me,' says Rex and gets up.

Malcolm covers his mouth: 'Oops. A moralist.'

'Tired,' says Rex curtly, and leaves.

Soldier finishes slurping her meal. Rex finishes Kerrie's glass.

He lies down giddily on the assorted rugs he's found, Soldier by his side. Starlight rains down as a light mist through the hole in the ceiling. Kerrie kneels down beside him.

'I knew who you were when I met you,' she whispers. 'You're the guy who sits in a corner and waits, because he knows some girl will come to him.'

Was he? Was he that guy? Yes ... probably. But was it calculated? He thinks back to that barbecue where they first met.

'I was going to get up for you, Kerrie. Offer my seat.'

'But I sat down before you could.'

He wonders who he actually was in life. Watching his life. Who was he? He struggles to wake.

'Why did you leave me, Kerrie?'

'Rex, you knew all you had to do was hug me and tell me we could make a life. But I was scared. I was scared that you wouldn't be there. That I would be … supporting us. I couldn't know the way the dogs could that you'd be there for me.'

Rex doesn't want to hear Kerrie's excuses. Or his own.

He wakes, tears stinging his eyes.

He returns to the top of the giant golf ball, braving the morning white of the sun. No one can hold the sun's stare. He scopes the camp. They haven't stirred yet. He surveys his surroundings more closely. Maps it out. From a map may come a plan. The outcrop he stands on descends thirty to forty metres to open grassland with occasional trees and shrubs, stretching all the way to the soldiers' camp. Dry lakebeds and claypans form giant stepping-stones. To the east, coloured sands. Behind the camp, further north, a rocky range.

How could he get drunk last night? He'd left himself and Soldier as vulnerable as this prostrating soil beneath the burnished sun.

He's becoming paranoid about getting caught. But the men don't wander far or do much. That all-day outing when they ran over the wombat must have been their last-ditch effort. He sees them argue. Arguing their options. They chew on buttons, cloth, anything. Hunger.

Their plight gnaws at him.

He sets up mattresses and boxes so he can jump down into the corridor if he needs to get down fast. He teaches Soldier a few times so she gets the idea. They almost end up having fun. He sets up two M16s hoping they've got bullets in them if it comes to him having to pull the trigger; he can't work out how to check.

He makes sure to bury Soldier's 'landmines'. He can't go too far. He wants to be the last man standing or … or something.

He runs out of things to do, things to fix. There are only so many times he can rearrange the piles he's made. His whole focus is in waiting for the soldiers to die. For the first time since emerging from the cellar, there is a pause. This great pause throws him back on himself. Before, everything was in acute magnification. Now, he is peeping down the wrong end of a telescope, and finds himself pitiful.

Also unnerving: there is a certain expectancy with Soldier in which he finds the germ of an accusation.

When he gets up slowly, she leaps up. When he climbs the giant golf ball, she follows, but sluggishly, knowing the destination. And, most grating, when he goes near the car, she runs to its front passenger door, pushing past the branches to leap and scratch at the window. Her accusation is plain: When are we moving on?

Before, he was chaperone to his dogs, endless provider of excursions, diversions, new places, pungent smells, stale scents. Now he has the one dog, and her whole focus is turned inward on him, a sunlamp with rays concentrated to a scorching pinpoint. He is examined and found wanting. Weakness. That a dog should be the one to suss this out in him ...

He should have shot Soldier and himself by now.

It is now sixteen days since his and Soldier's exhumation from the cellar. Or is it only fifteen? He's losing track.

One of the soldiers, Ross, seems to take his water with him and walk off north past the rocky range. Every day. It's become a routine for Rex to spy on them twice a day; in the morning when they're retiring and at sunset when they're rising. He thinks pointlessly about a new type of photography he would like to try. One in which the human figured. Oh, he took photos of his dogs, of paddocks, of windmills, of leaning sheds, but now he wonders if something was missing. He thinks about Jeffrey Smart's paintings of loveless urban landscapes, and the tiny figures in them. He remembers reading somewhere that Smart said he put tiny human figures in his paintings merely to give them scale. Was this disingenuous? Did Smart privately recognise another, deeper compulsion: the need for the human? Perhaps the universe requires consciousness to exist after all.

Rex scopes again. Four. God, what's happened to Ross? He knows they're low on food. An idea strikes him with a sick blow. A human who's not infected won't be a carrier. He gets to his feet. Surely not …? He should tell them about his stash. Maybe they don't have bullets. No, he's seen and heard them shooting. They have plenty.

He ducks behind his cover. Why don't they do it? End it? They're waiting, like him, till the last possible moment. He wants to gun them down, he wants to stop their struggling, their effort at life. His only fear is that they might shoot him before he shoots Soldier. And he can't shoot Soldier first because the noise will give him away. And besides, he can't shoot Soldier yet. Not until the last possible moment.

Oh God. He should go to them.

He looks again. Ross is back and he's with someone else. That pompous gait of the second man is so familiar. The figure, however, too thin. But then again, he would have lost weight …? Everyone has. Taking that into account … it can only be …

The others gather round him, all seeming to ask a single question. Malcolm shrugs. IQ cries, dejected. Ross observes all, impassive. Thor hits Malcolm. Tank points his M16 at Malcolm's temple. Rex starts to stand, with half a mind to holler. He never liked Malcolm but …

Boss waves Tank and Thor down, helping Malcolm to his feet. Malcolm uses his reprieve to vigorously argue his case, hands gesticulating madly, until they relent and he walks off. Where to?

So that's whom Ross has been taking water to … But where is Malcolm holed up?

When the others settle in for the day, Rex sneaks down the giant golf ball with Soldier. He arcs along one of the dried creek beds, getting a sore back from leaning over. They make their way past the camp and past the beginnings of the rocky outcrop beyond.

That's when he sees them. A collection of white buildings. What can Malcolm have been doing there?

Something bobbing towards him. Rex ducks down, pulling Soldier in and holding her close. That mop of grey hair. Malcolm hurries past and towards the camp. Retrieving his zoom lens, Rex watches as Malcolm wakes the soldiers in their tents. Motioning wildly, Malcolm points in the direction he came. The others grab guns. They all pile in the Hummer and tear off in the direction of the compound, leaving

Malcolm on his own.

Rex thinks about this. Malcolm must have worked out an antidote. He's done it!

Rex whistles with joy. He and Soldier have to take the long way back to avoid being seen by Malcolm but it's a happy trip. They set off underground.

He wakes to screaming. It's a woman's voice. He and Soldier clamber up the giant golf-ball. The Hummer isn't back but there's a new vehicle, a 4WD. Those present – Thor, Tank, Ross, IQ and Malcolm – have dragged a girl from it. They pull her into a tent. Rex ducks behind the rock, putting his hands over his ears. He can't stop the wailing. Soldier has her ears pitched, a low growl in her throat. He holds her muzzle before it becomes a bark, and peers back over the rock.

What are they doing to her? What? Malcolm walks away from the tent, into the bushes and towards the rise. He is hiding his face. They must be raping her.

But there's one missing. Where's Boss? The Hummer isn't back, either.

Rex paces back and forth. 'Oh God, oh God.'

He crouches on the ground. 'Give me strength.'

The woman stops mid-bawl.

Rex scrambles down the side of his lookout opposite the camp, Soldier sliding with him. They stumble through the webbed bush at the bottom, circling the rise's base. Now in sight of the camp, they leap down into the sand of one of the creek beds and hurry along, Rex barely bothering to stoop.

Rex intercepts Malcolm in the long grass.

Malcolm double-takes, shaking his head in disbelief. 'Rex?'

'You're not dreaming,' says Rex.

Malcolm stares at him. Up close, Rex can see the man's a mess. Tears seep from his eyes.

'Kerrie?' whines Malcolm.

'Dead.'

Malcolm flicks his eyes back to camp. He crumples to the ground next to Rex, Soldier sniffing him inquisitively.

'The girl?' demands Rex.

Malcolm explains she and another girl showed up in a 4WD at the compound where's he's been working. He hurried back to camp and alerted the soldiers.

Rex guesses the next bit: Thor, Tank, Ross and IQ brought back the girl they captured in the commandeered 4WD while Boss went after the one who escaped, using the Hummer.

The air is shattered by another cry from the tent.

'We've got to get her out tonight,' Rex hisses. 'Get her away.'

Malcolm doesn't meet Rex's furious gaze, but pats Soldier. He starts mumbling about something else. It takes a little while for Rex to work out he's changed topics to the virus.

'We took the idea from dietary hunger suppressants,' Malcolm says to himself as much as to Rex. 'Just reversed the process. As for the symptoms, rabies is as close as I can describe it.'

'The antidote?' asks Rex.

'"Antidote" isn't really the correct term in this – '

'You know what I mean,' Rex snarls.

'The virus has a protein coat which makes it more resistant to denaturing which – '

'Stop!'

He hates the way Malcolm excludes him with his scientific talk.

'Keep it simple or I'll shoot you.'

Malcolm glances vaguely towards camp. It's not much of a threat, because the sound of a shot will surely bring the others.

'Um, well, denaturing means … okay, for example, boiling the virus in water. That would normally kill most viruses.'

Malcolm descends into more mumbo jumbo – reverse osmosis and the like. Rex notices Ross exit the tent and look around idly. IQ stumbles out a moment later, throwing up. Rex tries to get the subject back on the girl but Malcolm only has one focus.

'Okay, but I thought you were targeting introduced species?' Rex interrupts. 'How did it get into humans? A mistake?'

Malcolm says nothing.

'Deliberate?'

He works his mouth to words. 'It was a species-specific virus. Rarely do viruses cross species. So yes, we made a virus that had a strong affinity for human cells.'

Rex stiffens. 'We? You *and* Kerrie?'

'She didn't know about the research into human subjects.'

'But she suspected?

'About May.'

Rex thinks about this. It tallies. Her sudden depression, her doubts.

He forces himself to ask these next questions. 'What did she do? Did she ask?'

'It's potentially a great weapon. Poison a country's water supply. Minimal damage to infrastructure, even better than chemicals.'

'It isn't much of a weapon if there isn't a vaccine.'

'That's a better word for it.'

'Well?' spits Rex impatiently.

'We were working on it.'

Rex glances at the campsite. Ross re-enters the tent. Rex considers: just because she isn't whimpering, doesn't mean it's stopped.

'Malcolm, when they go to bed, free the girl. Meet me here. We'll get away.'

Malcolm tugs at his once buoyant curls, now matted and plastered to his head.

'She has water. Lots of it. She won't tell us where.'

'Why?'

'Presumably it's a limited source.'

'How long have you got with these guys and your water?'

'Days.'

Rex looks at the tent then at Malcolm, for the first time noticing the bruises round his face.

'They've beaten you up.'

'Yes. They think it will expedite my research.'

Malcolm's eyes wander to the water bottle. 'Is that all you've got?'

What does he mean? Is that all he's got in terms of volume or in relation to a plan? Malcolm's stalling. Rex is going to have to do something. He can't let him go back. 'What are they doing to the girl, Malcolm?'

Malcolm says nothing.

Rex must do something. He must. He knows what they're doing.

'I'm trying to sterilise water at high pressure and with steam,' Malcolm blurts out. 'But they won't give me any more uncontaminated water to experiment with. I might have got somewhere if I still had the laboratory.'

'Why aren't you in the underground bunker?'

'We were out on a field trip. When we came back, the bunker was sealed. They wouldn't let us in, they wouldn't even communicate with us.'

Rex thinks it through. The bunker must have been sealed to lock the virus in with them. One of them must have become infected. In desperation, the survivors had then tried to blast their way out. That would explain the piled up furniture, the scattered limbs – the uninfected's last stand.

'What chance have we got?'

'None, Rex. Not since I lost my lab. Ever since, I've been stalling. And ... there's something else that's fundamentally wrong. Steaming the water should get rid of everything. Minerals, bacteria, *everything*. Maybe there was some sort of cross-contamination with Gary's research into the different physics of the multiverse. Maybe we've contaminated this universe with the mathematics of a parallel one, messing with the very core of life: water itself.'

Rex stares at Malcolm, perplexity and fear writ large on his face.

'What if I could – say, if you could miraculously get back in your laboratory?'

Rex sees the expression change on Malcolm's face, and immediately regrets his suggestion.

Rex waits all day in the sun. He can't see the girl. He can't even hear her.

Come on, man, come on. Malcolm doesn't come. Rex moves closer to the soldiers' camp. He worries Malcolm has given him away. But why haven't they come? Would they wait for the cool of night? Surely hunger would override that worry?

Malcolm must be wondering why Rex, by

comparison, is radiating such health. He must be wondering with whom he should throw in his lot.

Rex has spent years sitting back and allowing this hideous situation to happen, but now it is time to galvanise his will.

He heads back to the corridor.

Lying in his makeshift bed with Soldier, it occurs to him that it must be nearly Christmas. He's clocked up not quite three weeks of this pointless wandering.

He wakes in a sweat at sunrise.

They're eating meat on the bone they've roasted over a roaring fire. Malcolm resists initially, then sits down to join them. Soldier sniffs the air and steps forward.

'No, girl,' Rex whispers in disbelief.

Then: an engine. A plume of dust catching the sun. A dragon's cough. The Hummer pulling up.

This time he must know. He must do something. He must act. *Now.*

Boss has returned with the other girl.

He packs the car for an escape, keeping his M16, combat knife and sword on him.

He then ties up Soldier. It's a thin rope. If he doesn't come back, surely she'll have the sense to chew through it. She's chewed through bones five times its thickness. No, he's coming back. He chants under his breath, 'I'm gonna kill them, I'm gonna kill them.' Is that how it's done? Do soldiers psyche themselves up for battle? He wished he'd watched more war docos. He is trembling and sweating all over.

Malcolm is walking his way. Rex crawls along the ground and grabs Malcolm's leg. Malcolm ducks down in the spinifex with him.

'You have to help me, Malcolm. You'll be next. Now they've started, you'll be next.'

'Not if I tell them about your stockpile.'

Rex spits. 'Cunt.'

'They're my best bet now. With your remaining rations and this place those girls came from, I can survive this. You're just one man. Alone.'

Rex shakes with desperation. They're going to rape and eat the other girl too. He can't let it happen, this time he can't let it happen. 'We've got to save her, Malcolm!'

Malcolm bites his top lip like a child.

'Why didn't you bring the other girl last night?'

'They're my best bet.'

'For Christ's sake, Malcolm, we can't let this happen! Are you going to help me?'

Malcolm says nothing. Rex can hear her sobbing, her pleading.

'You're throwing your lot in with *them*?'

Still nothing.

'I know you ate the other girl, but did you rape her as well?'

Malcolm's eyes dart from left to right. 'She was unconscious by then.'

Swallowing drily, Rex tells Malcolm to kneel and lean forward. He throws him a handkerchief.

'What …? What are you going to do?'

'Tie that round your mouth. Then I'll tie your hands.'

Malcolm fumbles, dispirited.

'Tighter!'

Malcolm stares up at him.

'I'm coming back for you, ok? I just can't trust you right now. Now please, close your eyes while I tie your hands.'

Malcolm puts his feeble hands behind his back. Without support, he falls forward, his head hitting the dirt. His grey hair is so matted it is like it is in a hair net. He moves his hands forward again. Rex gives him a small but, he hopes, convincing kick.

'Oomph!'

'Behind your back.'

Malcolm leaves his forehead in the dirt and grass and puts his hands, his half-closed hands, once chubby like a baby's, behind his back. Rex takes a few deep breaths. Come on, he psyches himself. He could do it to that man in the general store. But that was instinct – the man was turning.

Malcolm's wondering what's taking so long.

Suspecting. His hands fidget, as if to invite the cord. Because the cord is better than the alternative.

Come on, Rex tells himself. The girl screams. This time he must act.

Rex peers over the bushes at the soldiers. They're in a scrum around her. They'll see the sword, not that they're looking his way. Well, it will only be for a second. He raises it.

Malcolm mumbles what must be 'Rex'.

Rex is nearly at their camp. He's crawled the hundred metres on his belly, armed only with M16 and combat knife (his cumbersome sword left next to Malcolm). A scorpion once passed in front of him, throwing up its claws in a theatrical shrug.

He makes it to the 4WD and sits up painfully. Getting his breath back, he edges to the front right tyre and lies on his side.

He can see Boss training an M16 on the others, who are in a scrum. They part to reveal the girl with her top ripped off. She pulls it up and ties it around herself. Boss suggests she get in the 4WD. Someone out of his sight must have moved because Boss suddenly churns up the dirt at their feet with bullets.

Crying from the car.

Good, good, he's got Boss on his side. Boss only came back this morning – he wasn't involved in last night's atrocities and may have thought he was helping by fetching the one who fled.

Rex hears Boss order his soldiers not to even go near the 4WD. Excellent. Rex waits a good hour, maybe more, till the sun gets to them and they each lie to fitful dozing under their tarps.

He thinks how to approach the girl? The hand over the mouth like in movies? She'll only yell out. He raises his head above the window. She spots him, her eyes widening, and he hurriedly holds his finger to his lips.

He leans into the open window and whispers to her under his breath.

'When I yell, "Run!" run to that large mound over there. Here, turn around.'

He leans in with his knife. She turns away reluctantly.

'Only when I say, "Run". I have a car there.'

He cuts the rope.

And ducks below the window.

A kid?

A moment passes where he can't think of anything else. A young girl. Couldn't be older than five. Was she dead or sleeping? She didn't seem to be deceased. Oh God.

IQ rouses from his bed. Rex stills himself. IQ sits down on a khaki metal trunk in front of Boss.

'Man, what did we do to that girl yesterday? What did we do?' groans IQ.

Boss starts up, a low rumble.

'You know what the score is. We's dyin, that's the

truth of it. You just postponed it a little, but died sooner with what you did. Might as well set back and relax or be done with it and shoot yourself. Hell, I'll shoot you. Could do with the practice before I top myself.'

'Hey, I ain't never toppin' myself,' says Tank in a deep voice, stirring in his hammock.

'I'm stayin' put,' mumbles Ross, also awake and edging closer to the 4WD. Rex hears the girl whimper.

Boss fingers his M16. 'You stand alongside of her, don't make her yours. Why don't you set down here and pray.'

A snort from Ross. Another voice. Not being able to see, Rex bets on it being IQ.

'What have we done?'

'Somethin',' says Boss. 'About anybody has. Done somethin', that is, they be ashamed to speak of. Let's not plan on revisiting it on those two. Move away from the vehicle.'

Yes, wills Rex, trying to curl up behind the wheel, *move away from the 4WD*.

'We need a hero,' says Thor. Sarcasm?

'Would that be you?' asks Boss, mocking.

Thor kicks at the dust. 'It might.' Definitely.

Thor sits. 'You have to sleep sometime, Grandpa.'

Rex calculates his chances. So, Boss is practically on his side, the way he's trying to protect the woman and the girl. And although it sounds like IQ engaged in the assault on the other girl, it would appear he's having regrets. Potentially two allies … But what is Boss' long-term plan, if any? How long can he hold a gun on Thor, Tank and Ross?

Not bloody long in this heat.

Rex rises up on his haunches, as quiet as he can, the strain in his calves unbearable. He peeps over the window. The woman is lassoing his eyes, imploring him to act. He shakes his head; not yet. She throws back her head in frustration, panic. Ba-room, ba-room, his heart beats, like an engine constantly kicking-over. So loud. They must be hearing it. It's throbbing blood-loud in his own ears.

Rex feels his legs cramping. Why did he come out now? Stupid. They're up early; they won't go to bed now. He tunes back into their conversation.

'We're in a wartime situation here,' says Tank, 'or hadn't you noticed? Over in Iraq — we pretty much shot anything that moved. Or fucked it.'

'Yeah, yeah, or fucked it,' echoes Thor. 'On them big battalion missions, it was a hoot. Those PSYOPs guys, they was totally fucked. We hit an IED once. You can get the slops, Grandpa.'

'We did wrong,' moans IQ.

'Man, you won't touch her?' teases Thor. 'He can't get hard, that's why.'

Thor and Tank clown. Ross claps.

Boss' voice. 'Boy, not much use in that behaviour. You set down here next to me, do you hear?'

'I ain't "setting" anywhere near you, old man,'

says Thor. 'I don't understand you. Why you don't do this, why you don't do that? Whatever gets you *on*.'

Tank and Thor high-five.

'We's the real deal,' raps Thor, before turning to the 4WD passenger window, Rex ducking below the driver's window just in time. 'We the boys with the big guns. I bet she'd like to hum on my balls. Mm, mm, hmm.'

Frightened whimpers from the woman and girl.

'You can fuck with me, my baby girl,' says Thor. From the volume of his voice, also at the passenger's window.

Boss yells at him to shut up.

With mock innocence: 'Hey, all I want's the honey.'

He and Tank high-five again.

'The baby's mine' – from Tank.

Rex checks under the 4WD: their feet have shuffled away. He peers over the lip of the window. Ross hasn't said much. Where does he stand?

'Fuck off. *I* makes the bitch wet,' says Thor to Tank. Then, grabbing his balls, 'I'm hurtin' right now. I'm hurtin' real bad. Before yesterday, I been without a girl so long to the test of man!'

'Why the fuck didn't they evac' us outta this hellhole?' moans IQ.

Thor tries to get into the 4WD. A scuffle then a rolled 'r' of bullets. Thor backs away from the vehicle. Rex tenses.

'You firin' off there, old man?' quips Tank.

Rex can see Thor thrusting his hips against the air.

'I'm fillin' her full of lead.'

'Ha, his links never run out,' laughs Tank. 'We don't ever have to worry about *his* rounds.'

Tank and Thor tussle. Tank pushes Thor.

'Man, smell your funk. Get off of me.'

'Yes, sir, this is end of times,' from Boss.

Rex fiddles with his M16. Why doesn't he shoot them? Mow them down here and now? Step out from behind the 4WD?

'Shoot me,' pleads IQ to Boss.

'Yes, please do,' Rex whispers, willing himself into invisibility.

'Keep facin' forward,' says Boss. 'My intent's to save the situation. It's wild and crazy. It's crazy. But keep facing forward. That goes a long ways. Lotta times he tells me keep facin' forward.'

Who? wonders Rex.

'Some of the bad memories. Someone all shot to shit,' drones Boss. 'They don't tell you, when you shoot a man, you don't always kill him.'

Shoot them, thinks Rex. Shoot them! He could reveal himself to Boss but would Boss shoot *him*? He could maybe get Tank, Thor and Ross but would IQ and Boss open up on him?

'War changes you,' intones Boss. 'This is what my mate asked:

"Is it true that the reasons we went, brus'
Aren't the same as the reasons they sent us?"
So I said, "If you and I were meant, Gus,
To know we'd not be here."

From Tank: 'If you're so smart, then why are you a soldier?'

Laughter.

Rex slides down the side of the 4WD and leans against the tyre. The tyre? He needs to sabotage their vehicles. If he gets away, he doesn't want them following. He unscrews the top of the air tube to the tyre, and sticks a twig in. It hisses. It can't be too loud but it's loud to him. Will that be enough? He gets his knife, still with blood on it, and fights the urge to vomit. He wedges this under the tyre at a forty-five degree angle.

They'll still have the Hummer though ...

When will they notice Malcolm's missing? He feels sick thinking about Malcolm. He'll never sleep properly again.

Legs cramping from not moving. The girl's got her hand out the window, tapping. He rises up. She gestures at him to do something, gesturing even as Rex is willing Boss to shoot.

There is no choice now. She'll alert them any minute. She whispers that they're sleeping. Still crouching, he edges round to the front bonnet.

They're all lying back on their respective hammocks except Boss, who's still sitting in his chair, M16 resting on his lap. How will he get through them to carry out his plan?

He sees Thor's Viking helmet on the 4WD's bonnet.

Rex thinks about some of the places he's taken photos. Places he wasn't meant to enter. He had his fluoro-orange safety vest and crash helmet. Even some plastic hazard fencing. He'd don the vest and helmet, set up a temporary fence and take his photos. He'd trespassed onto all sorts of sites and never had anyone ask what he was doing. The brazen approach.

With the Viking helmet on, he strolls casually to their plastic water container that's filled with what they must have got out from the very bottom of the tank. He unscrews the lid and glances round. Boss even seems to be staring at him. He takes a bottle from his knapsack, empties it into the top. There's a splatter of water in the nearly hollow plastic. Rex turns round. Tank rolls onto his side. Rex's tourniqued chest – how it aches. His indigestion heart. He walks back to the 4WD, each foot crunching on the dirt ground.

From beyond the rise, Soldier barks. In horror, Rex ducks out of sight.

Then he realises that he must have bumped the tap at the bottom of the container – it's now leaking.

'I dreamt about my dog, Cougar,' says IQ.

Tank gets up and turns off the tap. 'You been taking the water?'

IQ gasps. 'What? Manny took the water.'

'Did fuckin' not,' says Thor. 'But if you had some, I'm havin' some.'

'Stay away from that tank,' says Boss. Sounds like he was sleeping but covering it.

'Shoot,' says Thor, pouring himself a glass.

Rex can't help but feel overjoyed that Thor is about to be turned.

'I said stay away!'

Oddly, it wasn't Boss that said that, but Tank. Thor lifts the cup defiantly but Tank takes it off him.

'Hey!' protests Thor.

'It's *his* turn,' says Tank and Rex watches in horror as Tank hands IQ the cup.

Oh no, at least that one was showing contrition. Rex gags himself as he listens to the glug of IQ downing the glass. For a second, Rex sees Kerrie downing the glass, her last one.

Soldier barks again.

The kid in the convenience store.

Tank starts from under the shade of the tarps, in Soldier's direction. IQ seems okay. Oh God, this isn't working. He sees the woman's frightened eyes through the window, locked on his. Why didn't he bring a gun for her? He hasn't thought anything through.

119

'If *he* gets a drink, *I'm* having one,' spits Thor.

'Leave me alone,' stammers IQ.

'Here, doggy, here doggy,' from Tank, a little ways off, heading to the giant golf ball.

Why is nothing happening to IQ? It's more than thirty seconds; it's minutes now. Diluted? The contaminated water from his bottle is diluted in their tank? But there was hardly anything in the tank for his water to mix with.

'Hey, where's mah horns?' asks Thor.

Sick to the stomach, Rex lifts a hand to his head. Idiot! He quickly knocks the helmet off his head, comic style, and only just manages to catch it before it hits the ground. He can see Thor's boots. Thor's walking round the front of the 4WD. Any second, he'll be upon him. Rex raises his M16.

'Never eaten dog,' says Tank, some distance away now.

Soldier stops barking; IQ makes a grunt of pain; Thor's boots break in the gravel, in front of the 4WD bonnet. His eyes only have to wander down to his left and he'll see Rex.

'Hey, what's the matter, man?' Ross speaks for the first time in ages.

IQ doubles over then, throwing his head back, runs at Tank, biting into his arm just as Tank raises his gun.

Rex stands and shoots. He hits Boss. A wreath of blood roses blooms across his stomach. Oh God, of all the people he could shoot.

'RUN!' he yells to the girl.

The girl lurches from the car, the five year-old kid clutching her hand. Thor turns to Rex, confused in the sun's glare with who's who. Tank rolls free of IQ and opens up, IQ collapsing in a heap. Rex runs.

'Hey, Manny,' he hears yelled at him by Tank.

Then, some way back from Thor, 'Hey, I'm right here.'

Rex stumbles on a bush, falling painfully and grazing his knee. He throws a glance behind him.

'Don't … don't kill me,' says Tank, examining the bite IQ took out of his arm. Thor and Ross open fire on him. Not dawdling another second, Rex pitches forward.

In his reeling canter, he thinks about the Hummer. He meant to shoot the tyres. He sees his sword lying beside Malcolm's corpse and snatches it up before catching up to the girl and the kid, scrabbling round the rise. He overtakes and they follow.

Shit! The M16 – he dropped it when he tripped.

Soldier leaps up when he gets back. He unties her, trying to decide whether to go back for it. No, he has the handgun in the glove box – loaded with the two bullets he found for it. He hurries to the car. Pulling the branches off, he shoves the woman and kid in, and his sword under the back windscreen. He turns the engine over. It doesn't start. He's checked everything: water, gas, oil. He couldn't test-start it, though. Because of the noise.

Oh God, oh God.

He tries again. Success.

But the back wheels spin in the dirt. Oh God, oh God. Traction, need some traction. Idiot, he should have laid sticks under the wheels not just on top of the car. If he'd taken the 4WD …? But then again the keys weren't in the ignition. He wouldn't have had time to hotwire it and besides, he couldn't know it was loaded with fuel, water and provisions like his own car. The back wheels spin. He turns the wheel to a hard right and throws the gear stick in reverse. The wheels get traction and they're on the move.

He drives along bumpily, yelling to the girl to keep watch behind them. The Hummer's still stationary and soon the camp's out of sight. They're probably figuring out what's just happened. They've gone from five to three, with one of those three incapacitated. God, Rex filled Boss' gut with lead. He's heard being shot in the stomach is one of the most painful ways to die.

Help me.

The car rattles. He hits another sand bar, almost gets caught in its grainy grip. They get on the bitumen road.

They drive through the main gate. Rex jumps out. This bit he has thought out well. He snakes the high-tensile chain round the gate, and locks it. It won't hold them long but it's something. They'll have the keys to the lock but hopefully they ram the gate. Back in the car.

'Where are we going?' he barks at her.

The woman mentions the place. Rex turns right.

'What's your name?'

'Crystal.'

'If they catch us ...' he begins.

'Yeah?' she says and covers her girl's ears.

'Let's not let them take us alive.'

She nods.

'Mummy, I can't hear! Take your hands off my ears.'

'Shut up, Em.'

'I've got two bullets left,' says Rex. 'I'll shoot Soldier, cut your girl's head off, then yours, then shoot myself.'

She stares at him.

'Mummy, let go of me!'

'Shut it, Em.'

'My sword's very sharp,' says Rex then, trying to comfort her, 'I've done it before.'

Her features freeze motionless for a second before spasming. 'Shoot me dawda!'

Dawda? This throws Rex, but then he works it out: her strong accent is masking that she means 'daughter'.

'I have to do it that way!' he shouts back. 'There's no guarantee Soldier will stay put while I swing and then I'd have to finish her with a bullet anyway.'

Crystal stares at him, horror on her face.

Rex flinches with the memory of Malcolm. Malcolm had started to yelp, even with the hanky in his mouth. Rex had raised the sword, bringing down the hilt on the back of his head. Like in the movies, how it was done in the movies, only Malcolm rolled to one side, the hilt missed his head and the blade came down hard on his neck. It opened up with blood and he screamed a muffled scream. Rex jumped on him, Malcolm tripped, his head hitting a rock and opening up. Those eyes and the mouth bubbling a red, foam-tipped fountain. And then … well … Rex had no choice but to finish the job, using the combat knife so he wouldn't miss.

'You're hurting me, Mummy!'

'Shoot moi baby!' screams Crystal.

Rex, crying himself, nods in Soldier's direction. 'She's *my* baby.'

'Mummy!'

The girl is screaming now, bawling. Soldier leaps in the back and tries licking her.

'Fuck off, cunt!' demands Crystal.

'Up front, Soldier.'

Soldier leaps back, whining. 'Urrr, urrr.'

The girl's crying, Soldier's whining, Crystal's screaming. *Screaming*. Rex hits another curb, the sound seems to be getting louder. He is going to burst.

'What if oi ran at yous to get the gun off yous?

You'd have to shoot us then, eh?'

'No, I'd shoot myself. And then you'd have to cut your own heads off.'

He looks in the rear-view mirror, at the long stretch of straight road. There is a black dot on the horizon.

CHAPTER FOUR

So many snatches come back to him, so many little moments, which are big moments in hindsight. On an autumn's day, aged six, his hand cupped in his mother's. Needling cloud covers the sun and umbrellas blossom along the street, suns-spandrels. At eight, on one of those Sunday afternoons that seemed timeless, watching a TV programme he won't forget. Hiroshima blast. Men, women, children, their shadows caught and appliquéd to walls. His first gasp at the world. Sixteen, under a pine tree, a bed of needles, and a pale girl, lips soft and childish, watching him. Twenty-five, the collapsing accordion of detonated buildings. Thirty-two, sitting at a barbecue and a girl kneels beside him, Kerrie.

Recent memories, crowding out the others like a virus the body has stopped fighting.

The kid he poisoned with the water.

The father whose head he cut off.

Malcolm hacked then stabbed.

IQ poisoned.

Tank mauled then shot.

Boss' gut filled with bullets, a red cummerbund.

He tilts the rear-view mirror. That black dot is the same size. He adjusts it to see himself: in every mirror lurks a monster.

Why would he want this to happen?

He is walking as an eighteen-year-old along the suburban streets, his old, first dog waddling ten paces behind.

'Off! Get off!'

He turns to see his dog has been rushed off the verge and onto the road by a young man. Rex quickly scans both ways. No traffic. Very, very lucky. He calls his dog to the footpath but she is reluctant.

'Your dog …' the man explains a little guiltily, pointing to his lawn.

Rex is livid. 'I don't care what my dog was doing.'

He notes the guy has leading-man looks. 'If my dog had been hit by a car,' Rex continues, 'it would have cost your face.'

The guy steps back, tripping over the roses.

Rex had growled it.

His whole life has been building up to this.

They are covered in red dust. It is over everything. The car is an outside, mobile tomb. In the back seat, Crystal wipes the side window. He notes she has dark brown hair, dyed blonde, but the blonde has almost grown out. It is short and messy. That, combined with the heavy mascara that has run down her face in inky rivulets, makes her something of an owl. Late thirties?

'I have always gotten dogs so I have to live,' he tells her.

'Yeah?' she says.

'When this one dies ...'

She nods.

'At the moment, I have to live for her.'

'Yeah, oi see that.'

They are silent for a moment.

'But with kids, I would have to live a *very* long time. I wouldn't get the chance to reassess my commitment every decade or so. That's why I resisted Kerrie so long.'

Crystal says nothing for a moment. 'A good thing, eh. Way things turned out.'

He changes his grip on the steering wheel. 'Do you have a story for me?'

She blinks at him several times. He asks again.

'Nah.'

Is this his failure, that growing into adulthood, he

looked around at the world, read and watched films about the revolts before him and gave up? His generation rarely even protested.

He runs over a rock. There's an almighty crash then the sound of dragging. He hopes the muffler is still attached at the front. He stops, leaving the engine on and jumps out.

'Eh?' asks Crystal.

'Keep your eye out for them,' he yells, as he ducks down behind the boot.

Yep, muffler dragging. Duct tape and Baling wire would do the trick, maybe with some Beemans or Black Jack gum for good measure. He hasn't any of those.

'Coat hanger?'

'Eh?'

He asks Crystal to check the car for a coat hanger but he isn't hopeful. He knows everything in it.

He glimpses behind them, at the horizon. Is that a plume of dust? Hell, he can't just jump back in the car and keep driving. If the exhaust comes off altogether, they're stuffed.

He rummages through the boot, the back seat, panic – panic rising, infecting Crystal and Emmy. He steps back from the car.

'Oh God, if only I ...'

Fence. Hundred of kilometres of fence-wire parallel to the road. He checks the toolbox. Bloody hell, there isn't a single implement he can find to cut the wire. There are pliers, but they don't have that blade bit for snipping.

Bloody hell!

He sights the fence line again, then hurries to the weakest bit, twisting the wire back and forth, trying to make it snap. Crystal cottons on and joins him, working the other end.

He takes the length of wire they've removed and wiggles under the hot car, burning his fingers but managing to get the muffler securely back in place, affixed to the chassis. He thanks his father for those years they spent doing up cars, for the lateral, improvisational thinking he's acquired.

He allows one glance behind as he goes to the front passenger seat. The Hummer is plainly visible on the horizon. Crystal stares at him.

'It's good to go. Can you drive?'

She shakes her head.

Fuck.

He gets back in the driver's seat.

The road, the road.

Rex, fifteen, is with his mother at the hospital. Fluorescent green lights – too bright. Machine beeps and doctors being paged over the intercom. Industrial disinfectant unable to scrub out the smells of disease and mortality.

His mother, face the green/grey of imminent

death. 'I wish I could see who'll you'll grow up to be,' she says.

No you don't.

Crystal shrieks. He rights the car. A cactus of a tree passes narrowly to their left.

He is with Kerrie. About May, when she knew of the tests to make the virus work on humans. They are sitting without touching in front of their TV, watching crap.

'You never hug your father,' she says, during an ad-interruption. 'You are not a demonstrative family. I know you love each other but you don't show it.'

Rex is silent a moment. 'My mother was "demonstrative",' he rails. 'But she couldn't hold onto us, could she?'

Crystal pinches him. Rex forces himself to sit up. He must stay alert. The Hummer is gaining, some five hundred metres behind. They don't have any water. Rex has that advantage over them: water and food. He presses the accelerator but it is already down to the floor.

'I must tell you a story,' he says.

She nods.

It is a story he's nursed so long it has become positively baroque in the telling.

'When I went to visit my uncle's farm,' he begins,

'I naturally asked one day to whom the neighbouring property belonged. My uncle answered that he "would like to tell me not to visit but since this will make me the more curious, visit – only come back."

'It was a weatherboard, once painted white but now a crinkly grey. There was a porch, also the same dusty grey. The whole house was monochrome. Even the black windows had dusty lattice blinds behind their eyes. The property was flat and bare. Not even the effort at a garden. There weren't any decorative colours or brass numbers, just grey. It was thus to my surprise and first real trepidation that, having knocked several times without answer at the front door, I glanced down to see written in unclouded black within the foot-mat, the word, "Weakness". The oddity of this horrified me more than if the only writing on that abode had been "beware". A skull and crossbones would have made me laugh. But "Weakness"? I wondered then if the "Welcome Mat" was an addition of my uncle's, an obviously new inclusion in a derelict house. Would returning without entering confirm weakness in *me*? Was the welcome mat the owner's – if there was one – *own* idea? Trying the handle, I found the door unlocked. Weakness. Nothing now prevented me but that word. If the door had been locked, I could have left saying I was not going to be party to breaking-and-entering, but here I would only have to enter. Weakness. That word played on me with ever-greater insistence. Branding itself on my mind.'

'Weakness,' says Crystal.

'Yes.'

'Such is that incident's effect, or culmination on my life, that I hereby give it the title of my memoir.'

Rex checks the rear-view mirror again. The Hummer is still five hundred metres behind. Their desperate convoy passes through a small town, so small it's gone no sooner than they notice it, all the post boxes grouped together in one clump.

He looks about. Road signs sprayed with shot. An upturned trampoline, a summer's purchase. And a telegraph pole, wonky. A never-before-recalled memory comes back to Rex. Himself as a kid standing by a guy-rope on a power pole, using its plastic sheath as a javelin.

Up and down, up and down.

He turns to Crystal.

'You – you tell me a story.'

He notes her chest is heaving. Up and down. He tilts the rear-view mirror to catch sight of the girl with her mop of blonde hair. She's asleep. He spots Crystal turning her eyes from her daughter.

'Shoot me dawda … if it comes to it.'

Rex insists. 'What about you? You got a story?'

The girl stirs. Crystal quickly speaks.

'Me dawda's name's Emmylou. After Emmylou Harris, the singer. She's rool talented, but. Yer heard ov 'er?'

'No,' says Rex.

'Mummy, oi'm tired.'

'Shut up. No yer not. Dyin' for a cig. Wad yous do then?'

'Sorry.'

''Fore all this shit 'appened?'

Rex inhales deeply. 'I sponged off my girlfriend and, before that, sponged off my father. This is the most independence I've shown.'

Crystal turns sideways in her seat, eyebrows raised. 'Yeah? That's the truth, iz it? Fair dinkum?'

Fair dinkum. It was a phrase his father used.

'You got yerself a wife?'

Rex doesn't bother to say that he and Kerrie weren't married. 'Dead.' Rex asks in turn. 'You got a husband?'

She hesitates a second then: 'Yeah … same.'

Rex says nothing.

'Weren't a bad bloke. Didna wanna work like yous, but. Fucken lazy.' She pulls at her singlet. 'It's all these foreigners they bring in, what's done this, I reckon. We shoulda told them to rack off. That's why we's in this fucked state.'

'It isn't,' says Rex.

'How'd yous know so fucken much 'bout it then, eh?'

Rex closes his mouth. Emmy bawls.

'Close yer trap, sweetheart.'

The sky blisters with sunset, before turning a dark purple. Rex wonders if he can drive through the night. The Hummer is fifty metres behind. He hears a crack.

'Duck!'

A second crack and the back window breaks to beads.

He asks if everyone's all right. They're blubbering so they must be. He takes Soldier's measure, ears flat to her head and scanning around.

Thirty metres behind.

Rex thinks about zigzagging but that will slow them down. The gap is already too small. He considers turning off down one of the dirt side roads but the Hummer will be faster off the bitumen. He thinks and thinks.

Another crack and a whistle beside his head. A spider web instantly forms in the windscreen, a hole at its centre: a dead, black fly. *Perhaps he'll die ...*

No, the lights! He turns them off, hoping his eyes can adjust quickly. There is a moon, but only a half crescent, the paring of a nail tossed and stuck on the garbage bag sky.

For thirty seconds they're driving blind. And then a blue world, a desert under the sea, crystallizes before him. Crystal squeals. Rex swerves round the cow, the tail of a second thwacks across the front windscreen. In the rear-view mirror, he sees the Hummer's lights go out.

Pre-dawn. Rex is crouched beside the car in the wan light. He's ordering Crystal to fill the tank, check the water. And every few moments: 'Can you see them?'

'Emmy!' yells Crystal.

Emmy turns from where she's standing, five metres back up the road.

'Oi'm scared, Mummy, oi'm scared.'

Rex gets the last nut tightened on the tyre he's replaced.

'Mummy!'

Letting down the jack, he turns to Emmy. He knows immediately what her expression is saying.

'In the car!'

They pile in, Soldier having to be dragged from something she's sniffing in the grass. The Hummer is back in sight.

On the road again, the road. The road that is one snake, then two, then half a dozen slipping under and over each other. He turns to Crystal.

'Slap me.'

She hesitates.

'Slap me!'

'Oi, yous won't bif me back, eh?'

He nods no and she slaps him.

Two hundred metres behind.

The sun is fully risen.

One hundred.

What can he do? He shifts his thoughts to the glove box. The Colt Python. Stop and try to fight it out with them? They have rifles, automatic weapons, years of training. He has a handgun with two bullets. Shoot Soldier then himself and leave Crystal and Emmy to them? Thor and Ross are the worst of the soldiers. He killed Tank and presumably Boss by now.

Fifty metres. They'll start shooting soon.

What can he do, what can he do?

'Eh, look.'

There is a note of hope in Crystal's voice. He checks the rear-view mirror again. Is that smoke issuing from their radiator? Is that damage to the front? When their lights went out last night, that must have been them ploughing into the cows. Rex winces thinking about the poor creatures.

Yes it's smoke.

One hundred metres behind.

It's billowing out now.

Three hundred, four hundred, five hundred metres. He stops the car but keeps it running.

'Oi, keep drivin'!' yells Crystal.

Rex opens the boot, grabs his camera. It has the zoom lens attached. He squints through the eyepiece. The Hummer's stopped. It's billowing smoke.

Water. He cackles, momentarily unhinged. Their vehicle's dying of thirst. He gets back in the car.

'We'll drive till we're past walking distance.'

Crystal nods.

Seddon. Three days after he and Kerrie got back from Hamilton Island. Rex closes the boot of his car and takes in the empty boxes he got from the supermarket. Kerrie's in the lounge, sitting among her full boxes of books, clothes and knick-knacks, trying to decide which she'll keep at her parents', which she'll sell at the garage sale they've planned for the coming weekend. They're packing up to head to her job in the outback.

Her navy pilling cardigan is a size too small but she still has the buttons done up. It stretches in a zigzag pattern across her chest in a very fetching manner. The crotch of his jeans bulges. She has a cigarette in her mouth, lit. He puts down his boxes, crouches behind her and starts rubbing her neck, smelling the tobacco in her hair.

'I didn't know you smoke.'

'One of those men left his packet.'

Her shoulders remain stiff under the gentle pressure of his fingers. He must ask, although he knows the answer: 'Which men?'

She stands up and walks to the window, dropping the butt into a half-drunk coffee on the sill, reminding Rex of his father's same habit.

He takes her spot on the floor, sitting cross-legged. He can tell she isn't in the mood so he gets to the topic he wanted to delay. 'Kerrie, I looked up that company they say they belong to. I can't find anything about them on the net, anywhere.'

She nods like she's sought information on them too. Or tried to.

'I've been thinking,' he continues, 'maybe we should get a lawyer to peruse these contracts.'

She turns to him. 'Rex, I signed.'

'What did you sign?' he asks.

'The contract states that I can't even talk about that. I can't talk about my work at all. Ever.'

So much for her fame, he thinks.

After a car-trip with Buzz and Roger which they'd spread out to three days, he and Kerrie arrive in town. To Kerrie, the town is like all small country towns, with its sweaty pubs and modest monuments. But Rex is already picking out, and photographing, its differences, and Buzz and Roger cataloguing the new smells, all while Kerrie is pacing on her mobile, ringing her new employers.

She closes her phone with a click and says they are to wait at the shot tower.

'Where's that?' she asks, voice frayed.

Rex only nods to the highest structure in town. It's on a wide strip of dead grass that runs down the centre of the main drag, red-bricked, shaped like a chimney, with only three small windows evenly spaced at the top. Rex sits at its base with Buzz and Roger; Kerrie stands. A man in a wide-brimmed hat and frog-mouth, leaning against the shot tower, regards Rex.

'You follow the footy?'

Rex shakes his head.

The man beams foolishly; chews his lip; peers at Kerrie whose eyes are scouring from one end of the main street to the other. Unable to catch her eye, he turns back to Rex. 'Essendon's doin' well.'

Two black coupés pull up with black-tinted windows. The footy enthusiast shifts focus from the coupés to Rex and Kerrie before backing away. Two suited men get out of the cars, each wearing sunglasses and with one hand pressed to their ear-pieces.

Rex laughs.

The tallest looks at him, down to the dogs with their hackles raised, then back at Rex, his sunglasses reflecting the shot tower in duplicate.

'Seen *The Matrix*?' asks Rex.

The man continues to stare at him, saying nothing. A chill coming over him, even in this heat, Rex pulls his dogs close, patting down the hair on their backs. 'It's okay, guys, it's okay.'

Kerrie finishes talking to the other guy who then consults with the tall man.

Rex, with Buzz and Roger, follows the coupé that the tall man got back into, while Kerrie rides in the other coupé, behind.

He can barely keep up with the coupé ahead while the one behind rides on his tail.

'Fuck this … fuck this … fuck this.'

There is a fence passing by to his left. He sees a sign but hopes he's misread it as a rollercoaster lurches down his spine.

The coupé behind, with Kerrie inside, slows and turns off at the gate in the fence. Rex reluctantly presses down on his accelerator to catch up with the coupé ahead, keeping to the centre of the straight, bitumen road because the wrinkled sides break up into gravel.

The tall man shows him the house in a cursory manner, only flinching slightly when Rex calls Buzz and Roger inside with them. The house is oddly tropical in design given its location, with chipboard walls and cream linoleum floors, now grubby grey; and its bamboo carpets, bamboo partitions and even bamboo placemats.

In the lounge, one wall has been wallpapered with a photographed scene from a beach, replete with coconut-laden palm, bikini-clad dark-skinned girls, and white, buff surfers.

Rex turns to the tall man. 'Okay, I'm picturing that the previous owner likes Hawaii.'

'That's where the general has now retired.'

Rex watches through the open door as the tall man gets back in the coupé. As it drives off, it occurs to him he doesn't know if there were others who remained inside it. Or how many others were inside the one Kerrie went in, either.

Just who the hell did he let her go off with?

The afternoon is long. The house has been amply stocked with provisions, even alcohol. He feeds Buzz and Roger the two steaks and fixes himself a gin and tonic to go with the decoration but can't find any matchstick umbrellas.

He rings her mobile; it's off. He goes outside. The dogs scamper to the back doors of his Cressida.

'This is home now, guys,' he says, his voice betraying a slight tremor.

He turns back to the air-conditioned cool of the house. A faint engine sound; turning, he sees a black coupé. Buzz and Roger bark – he doesn't try to stop them. When it pulls up and the driver's door is thrown open, he's as surprised as they are.

'Hi,' beams Kerrie. She holds up the keys. 'Look what I got?'

'On loan?' asks Rex.

'No, it's ours.'

She walks over to him and, seeing his face more clearly, can also see his tightly-drawn mouth.

'No need to sweat,' she says. 'Gary and Malcolm have explained it to me – they're already here. Turns out our government only dropped the research publicly because of its sensitive nature. Privately, they arranged for our US allies to pick it up. It's part of the knowledge-sharing treaty between our countries.'

Rex remains stiff in her grasp.

They drive to town in the morning. Rex keeps flicking his attention to the fence on their right.

'That's where you're working, isn't it?' he asks.

She says nothing.

'So the Australian military and the American military are interested in funding pest control?'

Kerrie's eyebrows arch. 'Look, like they explained to me yesterday: the main purpose of the armed forces is to protect us. I mean, look how many peace-keeping missions our Aussie troops are sent on?'

The car is running dangerously hot.

'Are they there yet?' he keeps asking from under the hood.

'No,' says Crystal.

There's a small hole in the radiator. If he can at least keep water in it to a level that when he opens the radiator it's still visible, then they should be okay. But that will mean stopping frequently … What else can he do? Rex knows all the bush mechanic solutions. Eggs and oatmeal, but that can clog the entire system. And he has neither of those ingredients anyway. Could take a battery from a wrecked car, melt the lead in it to patch the hole? But he has neither a spare battery nor a soldering iron! He has very little to hand.

Okay, calm yourself, calm yourself, Rex. It's a small leak. Yes … but he should really wait till the car's cool to add the water. Putting water into the plastic tank as you usually would won't work with a leak, as it allows air into the system. You can check and add through the filler cap but only – only! – when the car is cool.

Shit, shit, shit!

There must be a simpler solution. His father would hit on a simpler stop-gap measure. He must think.

He's got it! Close the hole with the pliers. So simple.

They take five minutes to find them because Rex threw the tool carelessly into the back of the car when he took wire from the fence to fix the muffler.

It seems to work, but he really needs to turn off the engine for a bit. And sleep. God, he needs sleep.

When Rex next pops his head round the bonnet, they're still not there.

'Let's wait till they show.'

He hands Crystal his Colt, then wonders if he can trust her.

'The moment they show, wake me,' he says.

Rex wakes to darkness. He scrambles out of the passenger door.

'Oi, they never showed,' assures Crystal from where she and Emmy are keeping watch from the roof of the car.

He hops up with them, sighing.

'You done it,' she announces proudly.

Rex scrutinises the girl, Emmy, a blotch in the night.

'Does she talk?' he asks, but then he realises the answer: she's scared out of her mind.

In the morning, he rouses to see Crystal asleep in the back and Emmy sitting on the ground ten metres away, playing a game, her mother's straw hat nearly swallowing her gold head. Rex walks over to her, yawning.

'Do you want to buy something from my shop? Mummy already buyed a bottle top.'

'Get in the car, Em,' Crystal shouts from the backseat.

'But, but, but I don't want to. Powder brush? D'you need some makeup on you, Rex?'

Crystal, joining them, shushes Emmy. Rex thinks about the picture he must present.

'Probably,' he says.

'Sit down, please.'

Rex sits. Emmy waves a brush across his face. He shuts a door on a windy sneeze.

'There! My shop's closed.'

'They're not long opening hours,' says Rex, thinking about the long hours at his dad's café.

Emmy says nothing for a long stretch.

'Hey, *you* can have a shop,' she says at last, pushing a piece of wood at him. 'Where's Irene?'

Rex weighs Crystal's expression. Irene must be the

girl they captured.

'Will she be at the base?'

Crystal sweeps from Em's face to Rex. 'No, Em. It's just us, innit?'

Rex nods.

They get back in the car, and drive off. Crystal falls asleep in the backseat, Emmy wide awake beside her. Soldier is up front, 'navigator' for Rex.

'Soldia,' says Em.

Soldier turns round. Rex fastens Emmy's reflection in the rearview mirror. 'What was that, Em?'

'Oi'm callin' Soldia Rex and you Soldia.'

Rex says nothing.

'Soldia don't like her name. She likes Ruby.'

Rex stares ahead at the road. 'Soldier is the name she answers to.'

'She likes *Ruby*.'

Rex winks at her in the rear view mirror. 'But who will have Soldier as their name? If Soldier is now Ruby, you'll have to be Soldier, Soldier.'

'No! No! My name is Emmy.'

'But you like Soldier.'

'I don't like Soldia. I'm Emmy!'

'Then if you don't like Soldier, we'll have to leave that name with Ruby. Sound okay?'

'What?' asks Emmy.

They stop by a derelict weigh station. Crystal,

Emmy and Soldier get out of the car. Rex finds himself examining Crystal's shapely legs as she, Soldier and Emmy disappear behind a shed.

'She's pretty.'

'Don't do this, Kerrie.'

'*You're* doing it.'

He closes his eyes. 'So you *are* my imagination?'

'You're thinking about her,' says Kerrie.

'Is she my ghost too?'

Kerrie doesn't answer.

'I hope I *am* dreaming you, Kerrie, because when I die I want that to be it.'

'You're not a very romantic person.'

He opens his eyes, to see her sitting in the passenger seat beside him. 'How does that follow?'

'Believing that love lasts forever.'

'I'm surprised love exists at all.'

She huffs, exasperated. 'Rex, people much worse off than you are happier.'

'I know.'

He gets out of the car. Where the fuck can he be alone?

Back on the road.

Crystal has moved to the front passenger seat, now that Emmy and Soldier are friends in the back.

'All that schoolin',' laughs Crystal, 'where'd that get yas, eh? Oi was rool glad wen I was done wiv school an' that. Fucken borin'. If oi 'adn't lef' mid-way

147

fru grade ten, wouldna gotten a job at Coles. None of me girlfriends got one wen they was finished. Yeah, yous can bet I rubbed that in. Travel? Yeah, tried it. Wen' ta Malaysia, right. All these fucken moped thingeys. So fucken loud. Like a million lawn-mowers, day an' night. Only 'ave ta put up wiv that sundees, 'ere. We've got everthin' right 'ere. That's why they all wanna come over, takin' what's ours.'

'Who?' asks Rex.

'I'm Islamaphobic and proud of it. Them wantin' the same rights as fags, boongs and gooks.'

Rex blinks at her. He tries to erase those last sentiments she expressed: she could be very attractive. She seems to read his mind.

'Yeah, blokes bin grabbin' at me even 'fore oi got tits. So yer friends – thev got jobs?

'Most.'

Crystal's getting familiar now. 'So where was you wen all ya mates got seeros a foo years back?'

She pins him with her sardonic eyes for a moment then pulls down the mirror, dolling herself up. Rex wonders why on earth she's bothering. She looks across at him; appraises him up and down.

'You wouldna scrub up too bad wiv a shave.'

Rex stares at her a moment. At her singlet visible under her busty top.

'Ha!' she laughs and flicks the sun-visor back into place.

'Oi've got a special power.'

Rex glances across at her again. She looks away, coyly, doing her lipstick.

'Yeah?' he asks.

'Yeah. Oi can read men's minds.'

He turns back to the road. Sprung.

'Ha!' she laughs again.

Rex smiles to himself. 'So what am I thinking right now?'

'Stop the car an oi'll show yer.'

Rex stops. They both turn to see Emmy and Soldier asleep. They get out of the car, Rex grabs his tarp and blankets and they make their way to behind a bush.

They hadn't used condoms. They didn't have condoms to use. They're dead anyway, right?

He gets in the car first as she gets dressed.

'She's about on a par intellectually with your other favourite female companion.'

'Shut up, Kerrie.'

'We've only been separated two weeks, six days, eleven hours and four minutes.'

He's surprised ghosts keep such a precise tally of time. Strange when they must be forever.

Crystal gets in.

'Thank you,' says Rex.

She scopes him. 'You say fuck-all then sweet talk me *afta* I've fucked ya?'

Rex turns away. What he meant was, he was thankful her presence eradicated Kerrie's. But how could he explain that?

'You're welcome,' she says majestically.

Rex starts the engine, and turns the car back onto the road. Crystal tidies her hair.

'Oi, who's ya favourite singer?' she asks, pinning the longer tufts close to her head – wings at her temples.

'Chaka Khan.'

Crystal whoops. 'Chaka Khan? You shittin' me?'

Rex laughs. 'No, I ain't shittin' you.'

The car gets up speed.

'Me step mum, she fucken loves Chaka Khan. How old yer agin?'

'Classics are ageless,' says Rex.

She jabs at him. 'Yer alright.'

He wonders about the coquettish smiles. Who taught her those? He thinks back to the tree they laid under, the congealed blood of trees, prisons of light and insect life.

'This is me,' he tells her.

'Eh?'

'This is the man I am. There's nothing else.'

She leans her seat back, feigning tiredness. 'That's a fucken relief.'

'We'll be okay.'

'We'll be okay,' she echoes faintly after a snort of laughter, and then closes her eyes.

Rex insists. 'You, me, your daughter – us.'

'Craig – me last boyfriend – had kids ov iz own,

right. Fucken wen' harsher on Emmy, didn't 'e?'

Rex stares at her, genuinely perplexed. 'Why?'

She opens her eyes and lifts her seat up.

'You daft or something? She's not iz. She's moi dawda.'

Rex steals a glance at Soldier, Emmy's head resting on her tummy.

'Soldier – she's not mine, either,' he says.

Crystal stares at Soldier. Soldier wags her tail at her. 'And you woulda used yer last bullet on 'er, too, eh?'

Rex nods. Crystal bites back a sob. He reaches across and takes her hand. She lets him hold it a moment but he senses her discomfort. She pulls it away, pretending to adjust her bra.

'I'm sorry,' says Rex.

She stares out the window, at the smudged paddocks. 'Oi'm not a handbag, am oi?'

He shakes his head agreeably.

'Keep yer hands ta yerself till oi gives ya the nod, orright?'

He nods and stares straight ahead at the road, the road the bottom of an hour-glass, the sky an ever-emptying blue. Passing by, a few grass trees in their grass skirts, red spears against the green of foliage. Changing territory.

Crystal starts singing Chaka Khan out of key.

'Captured effortlessly.

That's the way it was.

It happened so naturally
I did not know it was love.
The next thing I felt was you
Holdin' me close.
What was I gonna do?
I let myself go ...'

Rex thinks of when he met Kerrie for the first time, at that barbecue, and he recited that nursery rhyme to her, 'There was an old woman who swallowed a fly,' and Kerrie joined in. 'I don't know why she swallowed a fly, perhaps she'll die.'

He turns to Crystal and tries to join in with her.

'Ain't nobody loves me better,' he begins then stops; he has found himself crying. I'm sorry, Kerrie, he thinks. Even though he's only been unfaithful to a ghost.

They stop at a lookout for a rest.

They take in the gum trees with their trunks in camouflage colours: white, khaki, blue. Their leaves almost an olive mist, when seen from a distance. On the other side of the road, a sign advertising the frequency of the local radio station: tune in.

They wander a little way down the embankment.

Trees with limbs looped with bark; like so many butlers' hands taking coats and scarves. Hearing human voices in the pops and burps of a nearby creek. And then the bush at night, opera. Crickets in the pit, with birds strutting and warbling on stage. It is a warbling mad music he wants to understand. No, not understand. Be part of, which would make the loneliness of trying to understand dissipate. Crystal makes a bed for the three of them to lie on. Rex spoons Crystal and Crystal spoons Emmy, Soldier nestled in the small of his back: cutlery for a four-course meal.

'Fish aren't really alive,' she says.

He is with Kerrie at Seddon. She is trying to find him something vegetarian to cook for dinner. It is long before she ever took her researches to the outback military compound, or signed any contract.

This time, this time he can make it better. He gets off his stool and walks round the bench to join her.

'I know,' says Rex. 'Let's save the world.'

She peers up from the fridge. 'How?'

He gently shuts the fridge and takes her hands. 'If I told you it was as simple as me going back to working with my father and you taking some unglamorous but worthwhile research job helping increase the population of pigmy possums, what would you say to that?'

She laughs. 'I'd say you were drunk.'

There is only the here and now.

'Why don't we get away? You and I tonight, beautiful?'

She blinks. He doesn't say things like 'beautiful' either.

'You think so?'

'We can. Just take off. Right now.'

'We can't.'

'No ...'

He leads her to the couch and sits with her, regarding her intently.

'I expect someone will come here. Escape to here. That's a funny thought, that this is where someone might escape to.' An inspiration takes him. 'Perhaps we should imagine for a night that we are new to this small spot, this neighbourhood, this house. Let's imagine the lives of the people who live here, and it's a boring existence, and they work hard, and leave for work early and get home late but, because it's novel to us, it's exciting, and we can see some glory in it, and intimacy, and faint, occasional revelations. Let's imagine we're this couple who've come home from this long day at work − only today, miraculously, despite the fact we rose at 5:00am, we are still filled with some strange, unaccountable energy, and want to celebrate this life, its grandeur, it's nobility but, above all, its honesty. Let's imagine.'

The tears necklace her eyes. 'Rex ...? Rex, is this you?'

'I hope so.'

'Rex,' she ventures, a sob in her throat. 'I want a family.'

But he wakes in darkness and screams into

Crystal's arms until Emmy's return scream makes him stop. Lightning neighs and bolts in the sky.

'Yous know what day it is, don't yas?' asks Crystal, patting his hair.

He and Emmy shake their heads.

'Christmas Eve.'

Exactly three weeks since he emerged from the cellar.

It rains and they forgo the bivvy for the car.

With sunrise, the clouds still coset the earth in mist.

Crystal bathing in the creek, Rex talking to Emmy in the shade of the embankment.

'You yelled at me.'

'I did?' says Rex, affecting innocence.

'You told me I'm diff'cult,' insists Emmy.

'Did I?'

'I don't like you callin' me diff'cult.'

'I'm sorry. Did I say you were difficult?'

'Yes, you called me diff'cult, Daddy Rex.'

Rex excuses himself. He makes his way up to the car and falls on the bonnet, Soldier at heel. He heaves nothing but the taste of bile. His heart thumps. His insides are going to split. 'Oh God, oh God,' he thinks. 'I now need four shots.'

Crystal is reluctant to leave their spot. She reckons they have a day's travel left at most. Rex wonders at her hesitancy to get back. She won't talk about the place or people that await them. He only worries that they are nearly out of food and water. They shouldn't wait till they have a day's provisions left before moving on. That doesn't allow any margin for error and his nerves are shot as it is with the uncertainty of each day.

He and Crystal make love in the mornings, before Emmy wakes. They all four swim in the daytime, making sure to restrict Emmy to wading.

'Don't swallow the water, Em,' warns Crystal: Emmy is in the shallows twirling her tutu of foam. Soldier muzzles the water as if launching a ball from the bridge of her nose.

They make fires at night, the logs a tepee.

It is the happiest Rex has felt.

Sometimes he catches sight of Kerrie sitting by the willow. She sobs as she watches Rex with his new family.

He calls out to her. 'We had everything we needed or would ever need.'

Kerrie averts a tear-varnished face.

Crystal's eyes rove from Rex to the willow, the willow with its golden hair, washed by the river. He sees its branches as a curtain of beads, its reflection doubling its height.

Kerrie fights for air among the sobs.

'I'll be with you soon,' he consoles.

Re-joining Crystal and Emmy sunbathing on the

grass, Rex closes his eyes and thinks of what is no longer. All the sprawling cities, their freeways an afterthought. He thinks of his and Kerrie's life in Melbourne, how – viewed from the Bolte Bridge – the skyscrapers opened like a pop-up book. How the motorists would tear up the inside lane, even though cars were parked ahead, the danger worth it to them just to get that one car-space in front. Millions of people who didn't know each other. Bridges with newly-erected barriers to stop suicides, ruining the view and sending them in front of trains instead. Cramped in the centre of town, Gothic churches, once the loci, now living in shadow, their crosses just one more road sign. Along the streets, hieroglyphic parking signs designed to confuse and entrap.

He thinks about the world they moved to. Piles of dead trees in the middle of paddocks where farmers have bulldozed them. Dead wood graveyards. And then the ring-barked trees, which are their own grave and headstone. In sparse front yards, the tyres cut and bent into swans, yet painted white even though we have our black variety. Between properties, a fence of pines, one side with a cowlick from the wind. Sheds made of cards, that shouldn't be standing. Windmills, their rotors and vanes the wings and abdomens of dragonflies. Along the roads, black shapes which are either squished snakes or blown tyres. Women turning at their clotheslines as you drive past, the sheets waving. In the small towns, youths espaliered to supermarket walls, beer bottles the colour of mud and cigarettes like chalk held illiterate in soft hands.

And the world, he, Crystal, Emmy and Soldier have known these past days. Amid the trees, freshly-dead branches, half-broken, hanging like bunches of withered grapes. Between their twigs, spider webs, skeletal flowers, open and close at dawn and dusk. In seas of grass, copses of trees are tropical islands. Tall rain like fences, forcing them into a shed. Percussive dinners where the tin roof applauds the rain. In the moist air, skinks on the corrugated walls stop to lick their own eyes, as if they don't believe what they're seeing: the world being given back.

A regression from city to country to bush life – or is it going forwards?

And each day, Kerrie, sobbing beneath the shivering willow. They'd had everything they needed or would ever need.

'And didn't know it,' she finishes for him.

He readjusts his back on the grass, reaching behind him like he's been handcuffed, to pull out a twig.

Which partner would Rex share the afterlife with? He feels a fear of death he never felt when he assumed it was nothingness. Now it has a weight, dragging him down to a central deadness older than any hope. He can't – he cannot – cope.

If the afterlife added up to all those moments in life of joy, those particles you missed, those miniscule moments of bliss … If life didn't die, but answered the why, insofar as it became …

Well, not the same. But better somehow. Better, finally, *now*. Not it-will-be-better … *some*how.

His eyes snap open.

'Dad, what should I do?'

Crystal and Emmy stir.

His dad doesn't answer; he's a happy ghost.

Rex lumbers to his feet. Kerrie looks up from where she is sitting under the willow's fringe, and mouths to him, 'Don't leave me.'

The horizon teethes the morning sky. They've spent one day shy of a week at this oasis. A month since he and Kerrie climbed out of their hole, and nearly two months since the virus broke.

Leaving Crystal and Emmy dozing, Rex returns to the road to check on the car. He picks at the white blossoms that lie on the bonnet like confetti. All the things that will be gone. Humans, in the great stretch of time, are but a blink. Dinosaurs lasted much longer, and they were reptiles. All the things that die with each person, and species. He rubs the white from his fingers. What meaning is there when nothing lasts?

The road, at last, listens: bark rustles in the wind, leaves turning over a purer literature. He tries to record the scene with his eyes and ears, his camera no longer between him and the world. The road, a curving blue tail, the bank a hairy rump. The telegraph lines (strings on a mandolin; their poles, frets) now carry nothing but a faint twang in the wind.

'We had everything we needed or would ever need.'

He sits on a white boulder that's fallen away from the cutting, and drags his feet in the blue gravel of the curb.

He remembers being a teenager watching long-limbed girls falling over and into each other with such grace and sensuousness. Envying their early puberty. While he and the other boys stood safe distances apart, envying the girls' closeness. The girls with fully-developed breasts while he had fuzz on his top lip. How the girls grew and changed, became different creatures, or their difference became exotic.

Kerrie crouches beside him. 'I knew who you were when I met you,' she whispers. 'You're the guy who sits in a corner and waits, because he knows some girl will come to him.'

They've had this conversation. He thinks back to its original iteration, that barbecue where they first met.

'I was going to get up for you, Kerrie. Offer my seat.'

But she sat down before he could.

He scrabbles down the embankment. Crystal,

dressing Emmy in a blue top, turns sharply.

'Thought yous moight ov left us.'

Are there tears in those hazel eyes?

Over breakfast, he asks Crystal to talk about her childhood so he can place himself in that time, so he can make the first move. Watching her and her friends giggling at him and his friends across the quadrangle ... But she dropped out of school in grade nine.

'Who's ya perfect woman, eh?' asks Crystal, looking up from her baked beans.

Rex knows he should say her, but he answers truthfully. 'Elle Macpherson.'

Crystal snorts. 'Elle!'

Emmy turns from Soldier, whom she's brushing with a Banksia nut. 'But, but, but L isn't a name. L's a letter!'

He laughs. 'We should hit the road.'

With that, he kills their brief taste of paradise.

They climb a gentle diagonal up the embankment, a paper cut-out of three people holding hands, ascending in size. He is smiling at Crystal. Her face changes to horror. He swings his eyes in the direction she's gawking. Thor and Ross are standing next to the Cressida.

Rex and Crystal crouch down to Emmy's height – her mouth is half open but Crystal's hand is already over it.

Rex sees a stand of pepper trees. 'Over there. Hide over there.'

Thank God they overshot. If they'd gone straight up the embankment to the car, they'd be right on them now.

Rex pulls out his belt and loops it round Soldier's neck as an impromptu collar. He'd been too hasty to throw away her old one.

'Take Soldier. Go on.'

She tries to drag; Soldier whines.

'Okay, forget Soldier. Now hide.'

Crystal's eyes plead with him. He nods assurance.

She and Emmy scuttle behind the barricaded cool of the pepper trees. Rex rises and walks towards Thor and Ross. Their backs turned, they don't notice. Where's their Hummer? They must have walked the rest of the way; that's why he didn't hear them. What on earth have they lived on these past six days? He stops ten paces from them, Soldier at heel. What should he do? They're drinking all the water, eating the last of the food. He listens to their listless talk, Thor standing, Ross sitting on the tar road. Thor has dispensed with the Viking helmet, having replaced it with a much more sensible wide brimmed hat. He wears a long-sleeved shirt and trousers, both a size too small. Ross is hatless, shirtless, with formal pants he's ripped the legs off. Both are sickeningly sunburnt, Ross to a caricature of human. Neither has noticed him yet.

Rex looks at his handgun: two shots, one each.

'Don't nobody care 'bout you out here,' says Thor, tucking into a can of corn.

Ross throws up between his legs from gorging himself, custard saliva on his chin. 'We shouldn't of left him, Manny.'

Thor burps. 'He was critical. Shot in da stomach.'

Rex winces.

Ross retches. Nothing left. 'He was a friend to us, Manny. For years. He didn't have nothin' against us. Not till what we's did.'

Thor throws the can in the air and catches it. 'Get up.'

'I don't wanna go home, Manny. I don't wanna look my ma in the face after what we's done. I didn't do nothing like this before. Wouldn't start no trouble. Mouthing off, maybe, at the po-lease. 'Bout it. Now we sick cunts and everything.'

Thor burps, drops his can and kicks it at Ross. 'We never do nothin' bad, man.'

'They won't say that,' says Ross, rubbing his knee.

'They?' wonders Rex.

'Whatever, dey got their own opinion,' counters Thor. 'For real, man. No, I never shot nobody. I don't stomp on that first girl's head. Honesty, no, deres gotta be more worser people than me, man. Everything is going good, man.'

'Judgement,' whispers Ross.

'Yes, that plays a part. But ... Everybody gotta do.

163

Somebody gotta act. Otherwise come chaos, man. We got enough o' that.'

Rex briskly walks the rest of the way to them, weapon raised. 'Drop your guns.'

They stare at him. Only Ross is holding his, a rifle slung across his back.

'Why don't you put him away,' says Thor to Ross.

'Maybe he'll do what he has to do, Manny.'

'I said drop it,' repeats Rex.

Thor sniggers. 'Lotta violence been done already, man. Lotta violence. You up for killing cats for real?'

Rex wants to shoots wide of Thor's head, but that will leave him with only one shot. He squints, lining the barrel up with his eye, its tip pointed at Thor's forehead. Ross unfolds from the ground like a newborn giraffe. Soldier backs up.

Sucking through bath-grime teeth, Thor sizes up the Colt Python aimed straight at him. 'Yeah, guess you gotta be, to last so long.'

'Please, ma, call my lawyer,' says Ross, wobbling on his feet.

'Mate, I said drop it!'

Thor leaps at Rex. Rex fires. Thor falls on the ground, a tunnel in his head. For once, a quick death. Open-mouthed in disbelief, Ross kneels beside his comrade. Meanwhile Rex shoves Soldier into the Cressida, chucks the Colt in after her, and then approaches Ross, feeling confidant he can get the rifle off him.

'Momma, Momma,' Ross is screaming.

Rex takes the rifle from Ross' fingers. Holding the barrel at Ross' forehead, Rex can't pull the trigger.

'Oh God, Momma.'

'The safety?' asks Rex.

'Forgive me, Momma!'

'If you don't tell me where the safety is I'm going to have to bludgeon you to death.'

The guy doesn't. Rex flicks what must be the safety. He aims it at the ground. It still won't fire. Maybe it's out of bullets. He'll have to use the last one in the handgun after all.

'Don't you look me in the eyes, Momma.'

Rex lifts the rifle butt – he can't bludgeon a man to death – then reaches in the Cressida for the sword.

'I'm comin', Momma. But don't you look at me, d'you hear.'

Rex puts the sword back and calls Crystal and Emmy. He can't do it. They're going to have to take Ross with them. He turns to collect him when an air-splitting crack rends the air. With a hot, wetting of his right calf, Rex's leg goes out from under him. Biting blue flint, he peers through the two front tyres of the Cressida at Ross also lying prostrate, peering back at him, two patients on adjoining hospital trolleys. In Ross' right hand, aimed at Rex's forehead, what looks like a Beretta M9. Rex reaches for the Colt Python in his pocket but remembers he threw it in the car. He rolls to his left, grunting with pain. Crack!

The tyre blows out next to him. The car dips, catching the next bullet in the fender. He waves Crystal and Emmy back. They slip behind the boot. Despite the more pressing pain in his calf, Rex's mind goes to the tyre. He's already affixed the spare. Maybe he can fill the burst one with spinifex?

He hauls himself into the car as he feels an explosion in his left foot. Where'd he throw that bloody gun? He pulls his leg in, peering over the bonnet. Crack. A wave of glass dumps over him. He panics for a good ten seconds as he gropes for the handgun under the seat before giving up. Sickeningly calm, he starts the engine, hand down on the gearstick, putting it gently in reverse. Crystal quickly pulls herself and a screaming Emmy onto the boot. Backing away reveals Ross in full, the bonnet dropping like a towel. Rex breaks, throwing the gearstick in first, Emmy and Crystal sliding off with a scream.

Come on, Rex, come on, he wills himself. He's got no other choice.

'I so ashamed,' squeals Ross. Rex knows if Ross blows out the next tyre, they're stranded. 'I was a kid once, Momma.' They're all dead anyway. He must kill so he, Crystal, Emmy and Soldier can survive that bit longer. 'Think o' me as that kid, Momma.' Come on, Rex. Ross holds the Beretta between his legs like a phallus. 'Forgive the adult.' Is Ross going to shoot Emmy and Crystal's feet? Rex tries to hit the accelerator but misses. Crack! The guy's fired another shot. Too late? No: no squeals, and nor has the car sunk. Where did that last bullet lodge then? He peeps over the dashboard. Ross has a wordless thought-bubble next to his head, coloured in red.

Rex moves in his seat to the sound of a squelch. For a second, he thinks he has wet himself. He takes a squiz at his right thigh. His trouser leg is sopping with blood. He then glances down at his left boot, slipping on the clutch.

The back door is yanked open. Crystal puts Emmy in then gets in the driver's seat, pushing Rex across and sending Soldier leaping into the back.

'Get his gun,' he says.

She drives, the tyre flapping, thut, thut. So she can drive after all? He rips off his shirt and tourniquets his leg.

'The gun, damn it.'

He falls on his side. The car bunny-hops. Beretta's fire nine shots, don't they? Soldier pushes her head between the seats and licks his face. How many bullets did the guy pop off? Emmy's staring at him, crying. Six. Perfect! With its three remaining bullets, and the one in the Colt, he, Crystal, Emmy and Soldier will have enough.

Crystal hasn't stopped.

But they need the three in the Beretta.

'The gun, babe …'

He blacks out.

He wakes up to the pain first, only then opening his eyes to stare at the roof of the immobile car. He works his seat to upright, his thigh and foot screaming. Crystal and Emmy are nowhere to be seen. The bandage on his calf has been reapplied with greater skill. Another applied to his foot. He spots a lone black tree: busted hat rack. He adjusts the rear-view mirror. His beard misses patches here and there. No one is complete.

He turns to Soldier in the driver's seat. 'You should have gone with them.'

He leans forward, spots a plastic bottle in the heat of the dashboard. She's left them water – why? To prolong the agony of their deaths? Strange sympathy.

'No, *you* stayed, Soldier. You stayed with me unlike Kerrie.' He reaches out a gaunt brown arm to scratch the sticky fur round her mouth. 'I chose right.'

CHAPTER FIVE

'Oh, Kerrie,' chuckles Malcolm, 'did you see that field marshal that flew in yesterday? She's officially my hot slut of the week. She has a boyfriend back home – vague nuisance – but I'm going to bed her. Bet on it?'

Malcolm reaches past the three-pronged candelabra. Kerrie leans forward with her braceleted arm and takes his hand. Rex focuses on their shake just as he remembers what time this memory dates from. It is three months after Rex found Soldier, and he and Kerrie have Malcolm over for dinner in their outback house. He's visited this moment before.

Involuntarily, 'Excuse me' pops from his lips and he gets up.

Malcolm covers his mouth: 'Oops. A moralist.'

Rex bites down on 'Tired,' the next word he said at the time, and stops himself from leaving, instead staring at Malcolm and Kerrie's faces lit from below by the candles, his clownish, hers doll-like.

'This was the beginning of the end,' says Rex, monotone.

Kerrie stares. This isn't how the rest of the dinner played out. Rex has changed the event. Malcolm dabs at his mouth with a red paper serviette before turning to Kerrie. Observing that she is focused solely on Rex, he frowns.

Rex leans onto the unsteady table, sending the candles' sundial shadows spinning.

'This moment,' he emphasises, 'was the end.'

Malcolm turns back to Rex, a queasy look of unreality on his face. 'You're talking about us as if you're in the future and "now" is memory.'

'I am.'

The colour is sucked from Malcolm's cheeks. Rex scopes Kerrie's. Hers too.

Malcolm picks up his glass of claret, which he shakes mechanically as though he were mixing a chemical solution. 'What can you mean, man? If this is your memory, you're saying we don't exist? Or exist only as this memory?'

Rex swaps focus to Kerrie. 'Kerrie, we're in limbo. I think maybe I'm dead too.'

Kerrie, her brown, unblinking eyes, targeted on his, whispers in a treble, '*Too*?'

Malcolm puts down his glass and stands up, pulling out the serviette he had tucked back down the front of his cravat, and daubs his expansive forehead. 'You're giving me quite a turn with all this, Rex. I must say, I didn't credit you with so much imagination. Your photos I concede, but this …'

Malcolm turns on the light but it is a low-wattage bulb and barely illuminates them any more brightly than the candles.

'Rex …?' mumbles Kerrie. 'Where are we *now* if this is "past"?'

Rex is glum; Kerrie makes an inhuman yelp.

'Not *we*?'

He takes her cold hands. 'No, Kerrie, you're dead.' They go rigid. He turns to Malcolm. 'You, too,' he throws off. 'I killed you.'

Malcolm crashes back in his chair, finger in mouth like a cork in a blue bottle. Rex examines him as if he's a specimen.

Kerrie wrings her hands, mumbling to herself. 'Then if we're dead in *your* universe but alive in *this* one …?' She looks up. 'Rex, why do you say *this* moment was the beginning of the end?'

Rex remains staring at Malcolm. 'Because I bet it's already begun: you've moved your research to creating a human-born virus. You, Kerrie, find out in May.'

Kerrie turns sharply to Malcolm. 'You told me "never",' she hisses.

The finger drops away. Malcolm stumbles back to his feet, jabbing at Rex. 'Hey, who have you been speaking to? You're in serious trouble, my man.'

Rex pushes him with a crash against the sideboard, the decanter over-toppling, and takes Kerrie's hands in his. 'Kerrie, I don't know why I'm back here, but I feel like I'm not remembering the moment – rather, I'm living it. Maybe we can prevent this. Maybe next time I visit a moment before you took this job, then I can – '

'Yes?' she cries, her fingers digging into his arms.

'Maybe we can – '

He's woken.

Blur of ceiling with an old fifties light, fluted frosted glass. A yellow cornice, crumbling. He's on his back. Old lolly-green walls, felt, the paper peeling. The light – very bright. Artificial or daylight streaming in? Artificial: it's fluorescent green, from a dentist's lampshade on the dresser to his left. Four out-of-focus faces in a ring above.

'He can fix cars rool good' – Crystal's voice.

'He's comin' round. Look, he's comin' round.' Raspy, familiar …?

'He very illt steel. Don't want we poosh him, not goot.' Foreign, Russian …?

He's killed five people,' says Crystal.

Eight, Rex corrects mentally. There was that father and son and, of course, Kerrie.

'Quite the keeller,' murmurs the Russian. A sallow face leans into focus. 'You can seet in feetures. Noteese the brow. Loo-ook, he starteenk to wake.'

Rex tries to sit up. Crystal leans in, hopeful.

'Rex?'

He mumbles his first word. 'Soldier?'

Her face crumples. He repeats it.

'Charge won't let 'er in the base. But she's orright.'

Rex leans back, then sits up hard. 'Emmy?'

Crystal gets her smile back. 'She's orright.'

'You?'

The smile broadens. 'Alive, eh.'

Weirdly, all four of them then wish him a Happy New Year.

Rex blacks out.

He wakes and inspects the room more closely. High ceilinged, cobwebbed. Opposite the foot of his bed, an ornate writing desk with its own hanging light, cosseted in curtained shade. To his right, a six-paned window with frosted — or is that dirty? — glass. Dirty: someone's played noughts and crosses on it. Crosses won. Must be afternoon. Or morning? Which way is west?

To his left, a higher, smaller window. Below that, shelves stacked with papers, books, all dust-covered. His bed, an old-fashioned iron one. It feels like afternoon but how can he tell?

'Do you ever think about me?'

Kerrie is to his right, sitting on a fifties iron seat

with padded vinyl cushioning, blackboard green, the sort of décor of which his father would approve.

'Do you, Rex?'

He hasn't thought about much else. Except for when he's been consumed with basic survival.

She lifts back her tweed skirt on her crossed legs to pick at a piece of imaginary lint on her patterned stockings. '*I* think about what went wrong. All the little things that added up to big things. I miss you.'

He turns his head on the stained black-and-white striped pillow to see her better. On her top, a frilled blouse, icecream pink. It occurs to him for the first time that in these visits she's always wearing something different. Shouldn't a ghost only have the wardrobe it died in?

She stretches back her skirt and gauges him in turn. 'Do *you* miss *me* or are you glad it's over?'

'No, Kerrie,' he says, holding the feelings down he can barely digest. 'I'm sad it's over.'

She removes aptly-named kangaroo paw from a beer glass on the small, port-stained, wood table beside him and dapples her fingers in the water. Water for flowers …? Given the dire shortage? There is something hopeful in this fact that he can't yet grasp.

'What New Year's resolution did you make, Rex?'

He stares at her, bewildered. What possible resolution can any of them make?

'I knew you'd leave me,' she says, putting the

kangaroo paw back in its vase. 'Although I never thought about it, I knew.'

He tries to sit up but feels a stabbing pain in his calf as the skin pulls at childish stitches. 'Kerrie,' he gets out, 'I think we can go back. I relive past moments with you. Are you there with me, or is that just my memory of you in those moments? Because ... well, if I go back early enough, I'll get you to destroy your research.' He gropes for her hand. 'Kerrie?'

'I don't understand these dreams,' says Kerrie, holding her ears. 'I don't, I don't, I don't.'

Her mouth opens into a scream he falls into.

There are no second chances.

A clock ticks in the hall, tut tut tut.

Someone has lowered the blind on the six-paned window. Afternoon or morning light seeps through the grime diffusion. The shadow from the louvres brands him. His right thigh throbs. His left foot, poking out of the blue wool blanket, is crag-shaped: no big toe.

A delicate hand daubs his mouth with water. It's troubling how Kerrie haunts him. It doesn't give him much hope of the refuge of death. Shooting himself was his greatest hope.

'Where's Soldier?' he asks.

How he loves to sink his hand in the thick

profusion of fur round her neck.

The hand sponges his face, neck, chest.

He can't quite focus on the face of the woman tending to him, but somehow he knows it isn't Kerrie's.

Morning. Another face leans closer, coming into focus, red raw with a patch over one eye. A spoon coming towards him, holding what resembles baby food. Corn-coloured, maybe even puréed corn. Rex recognises the face that was symmetrical last time he saw it.

'Well, if it isn't Mr Bravery!' Gus laughs, using the can and spoon as gesticulating aids to speech. 'Crystal said we had to go back for you. When she said the name Rex, I thought to meself, no way. And when she said you was a hero, I really thought no way. But who greets me at the car? Soldia! And who's in the car? The hero! The hero who wouldn't let me in his cellar while me mates got torn apart.'

'Gus, where's Soldier?'

'So you recognise me?'

Gus pulls up the fifties seat, flopping down in it. 'How'd I find this place, you're wondering? Well, I was in Nally and saw two of 'em raiding the combine for seeds. Seed packets when the rest of us is only thinking about water for ourselves. Not plants! So I tabulates to myself, they're onto somethin', and follow 'em back here.'

'Where's Soldier?'

'Charge can't abide dogs in the house. Eaties?'

Gus sticks the spoon in Rex's mouth. He tastes the corn, its grainy consistency. Gus sticks the spoon back in the can with gusto, the 'ping' quickly lost in the high-ceiling.

'Serial killer, eh? That's what Yevgeny, our doctor's, christened you. Rex, the guy who couldn't bear to eat meat but let his dogs eat meat for him. This mongrel left me bashing on his trapdoor,' he says to Crystal, as she slips through the peeling, red door. He then nudges Rex, to make sure he's listening. 'Fleeing your joint, guess what happened? Ran straight into a broken branch. I'm sure me skewered eyeball didn't go to waste.'

Gus leans forward till his head fills Rex's entire view. He lifts his eye-patch to reveal a half-chewed red.

Rex manages to make a gurgle.

'What did *that* taste like, I wonder?'

Rex faints.

He traces the word 'Weakness' written in black on the pristine doormat and enters the house. The screen door gently thwacks behind him. The air inside has been left too long alone: stagnant, unmixed. He draws in a chesty breath. Long soiled windows, some with the panes cracked in the centre, cast dominos of light. A drowsy fire struggles awake, the grate a protuberant lower jaw. Recent visitors? He slowly walks round, the black floorboards creaking. He tries to take it all in: coloured bottles on the shelves; a table lacquered with decoupage roses; dusty bookshelves crowned with wooden parapets; a black marble mantelpiece streaked with milk. There is too much.

Soon, all houses will grow dark at sunset.

He is visiting his mum at the hospital, the last time he saw her. She puts her hands with knuckles like budding horns on his hands, still young and healthy as reeds.

'You'll take care of the dogs for me, won't you?

'Yes, Mum.'

'Rex is getting on now – he's older than you – and needs his blanket put over him at night – he's got a short coat – and Tabs needs – '

'Yes!' He lowers his voice. 'Yes, I will, Mum.'

She pulls her tired hands up to her breast. 'I wish I could see who'll you'll grow up to be.'

He is with his dad sailing, the day after the funeral, on the catamaran. Rex leans out over the water. The hammered ocean has a depth he can't find in himself.

'Don't lean too far, son.'

The clattering sound of a sail being hoisted brings him to.

'Sorry to wake you,' says a girl.

His iron bed stops rocking. It is only the blind in his room that has been raised. Rex squints at the blossoming light, the pain in his thigh and foot waking with him. A young woman, in her mid to late twenties, sits beside him. She is thin, petite, with a ridiculously cute hairdo consisting of three ponytails half-taming her jet black hair in fountains; one spurting from above her forehead, another sticking out to the side, and the last erupting from the back of one ear. Her top has grey sleeves, the body of it pink with a transfer of a cartoon rabbit sucking its thumb.

'Hi, I'm Jenny Chan.'

She's smiling. The only smile he's received since the outbreak. She tops up the improvised vase – the beer glass.

'So you've got water here?' he asks.

'Yup. We're getting it from the tableland.'

'Why isn't it contaminated?' His mind floats out the window, into the cloudless sky, and answers his own question. 'It hasn't rained.'

'Crystal said you were quick.'

There *is* one other 'person' he's been given smiles from since this calamity: Soldier.

He grabs her delicate wrist. 'Tell this Charge-bloke, I want to see my fucking dog!'

She unlatches his fingers, stands up and gestures quickly to the closed red door. 'Don't let him hear you speak that way about him.'

He dozes. An hour or two later, someone is shaking him.

'Rex, Rex, wake up!'

The room is dim but he makes out Crystal next to him, her dark eye-shadow and messy two-toned hair making him, not for the first time, think of an owl.

'Oi, Rex, yous haven't told Charge 'bout us, eh?'

What can she be on about?

''Ave ya?'

He shakes his head. 'Where's Soldier?'

She moans – in relief, turmoil? – clutches his hand, kissing it.

'How could it possibly matter?' he asks.

She glances up at him, her eyes wide. 'Charge, he's moi husband.'

Jenny finishes helping him back from the bathroom.

'I've been giving Soldier scraps,' she says, when she's got him lying down.

He takes her hand and cries, rubbing blood into her delicate skin.

'Can I tell you a story?' he asks, once he's composed himself.

She gives him a look like she can't stay long but nods, trying to reclaim her hands.

Rex clears his throat. 'I went into my yard late at

night and thought I saw a large, skinny dog with malformed or broken limbs. It tried to stand up.

'"It's okay," I said. "It's okay."

'It stayed but unfurled and stood up. To my surprise and shock, I realised that it was not a dog but a young man, wearing a furry costume. The costume was so worn, and so dirty, that whole tufts were missing in some places, while the fur in others was matted together in dark glistening patches. He clearly hadn't taken off the costume in a very long time. His beard grew irregularly as if his jaw were covered in scars.

'I inquired into his life, amazed. His speech was faltering, and patchy, like the fur on his costume. He simply reassured himself through various questions of me that I would do him no harm. He mentioned the veranda at the back of my shed that he and his friends were aware of as a possible shelter. There were others with this lifestyle? They just weren't sure what my response would be if I ever caught them.

'I asked him what he did for food. He mumbled that there was food aplenty if one knew where to target. And, besides, his mother still left out food for him twice a week.

'This particularly affected me. I tried to imagine how his mum coped with this alien lifestyle of her son's. As he left, two other shapes moved out from under the bushes – feral dog creatures such as himself but not yet quite so transformed. One of them still wore jeans – tatty, filthy jeans but an item of human clothing nonetheless.

'As he left with his friends, he told me to check their website and gave me the address. This truly confused me – vagrancy *and* websites? I made myself remember that website as I woke up. My effort to remember that website woke me up. I though I had it and could catch out a dream. But it was nonsense.'

Rex lets go of her hand. 'All nonsense, you see. You got a story for me?'

She kneads her hand. 'Not like that.'

She lifts up a leg and hugs it to herself.

'It's okay,' he says. 'I'm not mad. At least not completely.'

This gets a half smile.

'You take photos?' she laughs. 'That's so cool!' For magazines and papers?'

Took photos, thinks Rex. Why is she stuck in the present tense?

'Not often,' he answers finally.

'Wow.'

He's touched she's still impressed. 'What did *you* do?'

She slaps her knee. 'Oh no! You'll find it wa-a-ay boring after that.'

'Tell me.'

'I work in environmental sustainability.' She pulls her shirt up over her mouth. 'Sounds wanky, I know,' comes out muffled.

No it doesn't, thinks Rex. 'Go on.'

She uncovers her mouth. 'Well, finding which seeds to plant, more economic, water-efficient ways to grow crops. I'm a real nerd. I mean, look at me! That's what I was doing up here, regenerating indigenous flora and fauna. Looking at salination. Building up mounds and planting trees on them to get their roots away from the salt we've dredged up. That sort of thing. That's how I knew how to tap the tableland. We were testing the water down there anyway.'

'We?'

'Well, just me now. They …' For the first time he's known her, her face clouds over with her own dark memories, clearing almost as quickly. 'But a photographer – that's so cool.'

This time she takes *his* hand. 'Crystal's lucky to have Charge, although he's a bit scary.' She bites her lip. 'I didn't think a guy would show up *I'd* like.'

She beams winsomely. Rex returns the smile, squeezing her hand.

'It was you – you who gave me water and washed me?'

She blushes.

A fear overcomes Rex, a need for ultimate meaning he'd long since stopped caring about. His father was, in his father's own estimation, a 'casual Christian'. It wasn't something he mentioned much, but it was there. In contrast to his father, Rex had stumbled on that greatest stumbling block to belief, the problem of suffering. To him, the nature of the world refuted the existence of a caring God. And an uncaring God was beyond contemplating. The idea of an omnipotent, benevolent being tallying good and bad deeds that were righted in heaven seemed optimistic when held against the wrongs never righted on earth. Without anyone left to worship Him, would God still exist if He ever had? Who requires their personal pronoun to be capitalised anyway?

'That's *our* doing, not God's,' says his father, cigarette in hand, ashing into an empty can of whisky and dry, he and Rex sitting in the courtyard of the café.

'What *is* God's doing then?' asks Rex.

Not getting an answer, he asks Jenny.

'I'm Buddhist.'

'So this is karma?'

She laughs then slaps his chest. 'Yeah, we must've done some wa-a-ay bad stuff to end up here!'

Rex pulls the baby blue hospital grade blanket to his chin. Jenny leans back, crossing the other leg.

'So-o-o,' says Rex, playfully copying her tone, 'you

believe we'll keep living over our lives in an infinity of universes till we get it right?'

She depresses her nose like it's a button. 'Something like that.'

His shoulder brushes against splinters in the busted doorjamb – tiny harpoons, uncoiling thread. Yevgeny enters and tut tuts, leading him back to bed.

'Vare are you goink, Rex? The truth is, I can't leet you go. Somevun so youseful. You very bet character: serial keeller!' Yevgeny plumps the pillows and pulls back the blanket. 'You goot Charge strutting chest, dah. He's thin-kin ten he's killt. But what ex-cites me weeth your tally, Rex: half waren't Turned.'

Yevgeny heads to his trolly, a whirlpool of instruments. Rex stares at him, a big, lumbering man, thick goggles for glasses, pimply painful-looking skin. Lank, black hair streaked with grey. A stoop, and a smell of fermented sweat. He returns with a pink washcloth, somewhat cartoonish against his appearance.

'Barefore zis, my life ware very goot. My wife – me – was normal people. Wife ware doctor. Terapist. Lived in Melbourne. Very ex-cited. I lurved there. I cam-ed here nineteen hundred ninety five. Moscoe, then, how you say? Opposite of goot. I hat three dreams, may-be four. Not shy. I dream about literature – I do it, I write. To be traveller, to see all the werld. I travellt America three times with my fairvorit wife. Here, worsh your face.'

Rex takes the washcloth.

'Australia change-jed me very much, very deefirent. But now zis, very fewteel situation.'

Rex tugs at the bandage on his thigh.

'A prognosis on leg? All things considerate, very goot. I conteenue.'

'It hurts,' says Rex.

'I fix-ed it well. You have very slight limp, that is all.'

Rex lays back on his bed. Yevgeny sneezes like a horse, spraying Rex with snot. *Fuck it*, thinks Rex, and tries to get up.

'Wat are you doink? Stay poot. I assyoom you steel very tired? Not time you strote around. You'll coal-ups on floor. Very bet conseequinces. Ware you goink, anyway? Not many opeshuns else, dah? Not likk barefore! We brought this on ourselves. We undereestimated, devalue-ed, let us say, worter. This is worter's re-venge. Our makeup is most worter. The body revolts against eetself. There is poetry in it, dah? Such remnants as we.'

Yevgeny lays his hands on Rex's calf. 'Does it hert? What rate your pain out ofe ten?'

'Five.'

'Five? A meer pass? Not seven or eet? Coo-ed you not underquote, Rex. I conteenue.'

Yevgeny twists Rex's leg in such a way that Rex

grunts seven.

'We can do better, I theenk.'

Yevgeny fingers the bullet hole in Rex's calf. Rex's eyes roll back to white as he screams.

'Dah, dah, you live! You live!'

Rex is at the embankment where he spent a week with Crystal and Emmy. It's early, frosty morning.

He takes a leak on a straggly salt-bush, telling Soldier to get out of the way. When he's done, she crouches and pisses on the same spot. This makes him start. Erasing his presence?

He calls her, trembling, but she doesn't come.

'Where's Soldier?'

Pitch black. The stars must be blanketed in cloud. He tries to roll on his bad side and winces. Kerrie. He thinks back to nights he went out dancing with her. He thinks also of previous girlfriends. Two serious ones. Such closeness they shared only for that closeness to go. When they broke up, they never saw each other again. Girls he thought of every day, then every couple of days, every week, month, then years passed. After such closeness, such distance.

What matters if it doesn't last? He thinks of dancing, dancing with girls, drinking with his male friends, joints, ecstasy, times of such closeness. And now such distance. Who he was, who he is now. What can we keep of others, when we retain so little of ourselves? An anxiety of remembrance floods Rex with a strength of nostalgia he has never felt before. He turns to the pillow and weeps. Oh God, oh God, it will all be gone. One might as well endeavour to cup sand in the surf. All this will be gone.

What has he computed? What has he made of it all but to be done with it before he properly got started? Help me, he laments to pillow. The lives he's intersected imperfectly, rarely colliding, mostly glancing off. Who has he been? Was it fear of embarrassment that made his life a long hesitation? A pose that was mainly weakness? He'll die. One day he won't exist. And potentially being the last, he will bring to fruition what he once thought would be his greatest triumph.

He won't be missed.

'Loving Kerrie,' he sings, swivelling her around, light paddling them with its daddy-long-legs through the leaves above. Getting dizzy, they fall on the leaf-littered grass, Rex placing his head on her lap. He fingers a key-shaped hole in her stocking. 'Let's have friends round.'

Looking up, her expression disturbs him but he won't be defeated. 'Kerrie,' he beams, sitting up, 'let's live a little.'

She stares back at him. Undeterred, he gets to his feet.

'Kerrie, if you knew we haunted the land when

dead, how would you wish to leave it?'

'I see you've got your shadow,' says Kerrie.

'My shadow?'

'Soldier.'

His gaze flicks to Soldier. She is even standing on the side to him opposite the sun. An axe cleaves his heart: this memory is too late. It is when he spent those days at the creek with the truck filled with tins of tomato.

Kerrie is already dead.

He wakes, Jenny with him, trying to get him to roll on his other side.

'Where's Soldier?'

If he could go back and live his life – not observe. He quickly gets back into the dream before it's gone; this is his chance.

They're at her house in Seddon, only Buzz and Roger for company. Before Kerrie took the job in the outback. Before any of this. He's done it! He'll stop her.

No.

Wait.

A horrible thought. If he changes their course, does that mean he'll lose Soldier? Never meet her? For everything, a cost! The world or Soldier?

He and Kerrie are rugged up on the couch, not even the TV has got between them yet, Buzz and

Roger spreadeagled on the carpet next to the fire.

No Soldier.

He has to decide, he has to decide now. If he changes their course, who will pick her up along that nameless stretch of road? His eyes prick with tears.

Goodbye, Soldier.

He fervently tells Kerrie how she mustn't take the job. How she should end her research. How he'll take his share of responsibility, get a job, care for them. He talks and talks until she has stopped trying to interrupt and merely stares at him. In the back of his head, he's thinking he can still take that road trip to find Soldier. He'll have everything; they *had* everything; they will have all that again.

Kerrie blinks her long black lashes at him.

'You're pretty,' says Rex.

Kerrie blushes. 'Rex doesn't say that.'

'Who's he?' he laughs. 'I found you pretty, and I wanted to be in your arms, snugly, eternally. That's what I should have said. That's what we should have meant to each other. I'm sorry for everything that got in the way of life, that's anti-life, that doesn't matter. Much of it was already here to prevent us, some of it we brought with us, but most of it we could have shielded ourselves from with each other, with an embrace.'

She seems to relent for a moment then: 'Don't go artistic on me. I'm taking this job.'

'No, no, Kerrie,' he cries as he is sucked up. Sucked

up into the light, which is no light at all, but an ostentatious darkness.

It takes a while for Rex to see the man but when he does he gets the icy feeling he's been standing there a long time. He immediately knows who he is.

'Charge is the name. Pissfartin's the game. 'Ere – 'ave anuver coffee if don' kep ya too awake.'

Rex has been recovering for five days – that's how long it's taken to meet this guy, how long Soldier's been locked outside. Rex has wanted to ask Crystal whether she took his Colt from the Cressida or if it's still under the seat. What he wouldn't do for it now. But he hasn't had the chance. This silhouette before him must have monopolised her time. Charge steps into the light and hands Rex a chipped mug. Muscularly handsome. A shaved head, well-shaped. Square jaw, pricked in blonde stubble. A profusion of tatts. Scars on his arm.

Rex cradles the lukewarm coffee, and also notes Charge's strong wrists and biceps.

'Where's Soldier?' he asks.

Charge takes the fifties chair, swivels it round in one hand and sits on it with the backrest in front so he can cross his tattooed arms over it.

'Yer got yerself plans for tonight, Rex?'

Rex just wants Soldier let in. Charge answers his own question.

'What am *oi* gonna do? Oi iz gonna watch footy on

191

TV an' oi moit 'ave a foo longnecks too. Sum ov me mates moight come round. Then mabes we go down the races but dey won't be there, will they, fucked carnts, cos dey got locked up da nite before, didn' they? Yeah, oi wish! Nah, dey won't be dere, 'cause dere all fucken dead, aren't they?'

Rex stares at him. Charge rides the chair along the wood floor till the backrest is pressed right up against the mattress.

'Now what *yous* gonna do?

Rex slightly shifts, his calf throbbing. Is this a challenge? To his great annoyance, his wounded leg starts to shake. Charge stares at the trembling sheet and sneers cruelly.

'To be or not to be, innit?'

Rex cocks his head.

'You bin asking doc for a gun. Thinkin' 'bout toppin yerself, yer mad cunt?'

The door starts to open. Charge yells. 'Fuck youselves, the lot of yous! I'm totally with daft-features and niggers be brown here.'

A red face pokes through.

'Nah, you can come in, Gus me boy. You can come in.'

The two stare at each other a moment before Charge grins.

'Gus got some uncomplimentary things ta say 'bout yer, Rex.'

Rex licks at his already dry lips. Gus sits down

heavily on the bed, forcing Rex to move back closer to Charge. Sweat jewels Rex's forehead.

'Hey, Charge!' laughs Gus. 'Got a funny story about Rex, I have. You'll love this one. Wanna hear?'

Staring at Rex, Charge grins and nods. Rex quickly trawls through what the story might be.

'I was in the bottle-o with this mad bastard, and what does Henrietta say? The sheila that runs the joint? She says, "You spend a lot." Rex, here, replies, all innocent-like, 'Do I?' Know what she says next? 'So-o-o, are you married?'

Gus and Charge laugh.

'Aw, Christ, Charge, these bastards, the money was drippin' out of them. Them and their rich set from the base. You should've seen them. Facelifts on some of 'em. The skin pulled tight. They were so tight, they couldn't shit. It was so classical to see the top brass wearing these suits. One bloke, he musta grew into it. No way you would've pulled it over that ego.'

Gus pulls a hip flask from his jacket and pours a dose into Rex's coffee. 'That'll put fur on your tonsils.'

Rex takes a small swig and splutters. Gus and Charge laugh.

'Something Yevgeny concocted,' says Gus. 'Our bootlegging doctor. Well, guess I should be gettin' back to work. Plantin' trees. You know, burying 'em up to the neck. Still knock into walls from time to time. Hard when you've lost half your vision. I go by the stars. They're a bit more reliable than your brain.'

Charge barks for Gus to stay. Obediently, Gus sits back down on the bed.

Charge leans in. 'Hear ya likes yer cars, Rex?' Me, oi drive a Daddo 180-B. "Aussie patriot" on me numberplate. Oi've got proud convict blood, see. Winston Churchill said "Defend to the death our native soil, our island home." Australia, love it or the get the fuck out! That last bit's pure Charge.'

Gus slaps his thigh. 'By Jingo, couldn't agree more, Charge me mate! War memorials – I take them seriously. By Christ, you've got to. Those young lads – wasn't for them, you young blokes'd all have slanty eyes by now.'

Rex blinks.

'Christ, they want our country, Jenny Chan's lot.'

Rex finally gets a sentence out. 'Jenny Chan likes you, Gus.'

Gus looks churlish. Charge stands, knocking over the chair which he doesn't bother to pick up. 'Don't give me no two cunts 'bout racism in any of its multifarious splendours, shit for cunting brains. Coon Yi helpin' Gus? No fucken way. *We* help *them*. Sent Crystal and Irene out for one simple job. Supplies. Irene, a curry-muncher from the Turd Fucken World. From what I hears, couldn't string a sentence togeva even ta save 'er from death rape. Pity innit? ... *Not*. You implyin' one ov me mates is shackin' up with one? Prince Dirt, you really are a two-faced cunt, aren't ya? You got somewheres else ta go play, ya whiny cunt?'

Rex scans about fruitlessly. There is nothing he can use as a weapon. This guy's built like a bull – he'd be overpowered in seconds. Gus is looking sheepish, wringing his hands.

'Well, Charge me mate, let's leave this yellow bastard. Get back to work.'

'Yous callin me a slack cunt?' Charge spits at Gus. 'Fink ya? Nah, oi'm gonna get somewheres wid totally daft features and fucked up multifarious splendours on dis ere one.' Charge faces Rex. 'From what oi hears, Prince Dirt, bud, Prince Dirt had a pretty good time out there, didn't ya, ya feral fuck? Yeah, you do that, av anuva coffee.'

Oh God, oh God, thinks Rex, the mug shaking in his hands. Why is this Charge guy getting so riled up? Perhaps he knows about him and Crystal sleeping together. Rex didn't know she was married! She said her husband was dead! *He'd* wish a partner dead if it was Charge.

'Oi moit av a foo longnecks meself. If there was fuckin any!'

Charge saunters to the window, legs out wide, muscled arms held out from his body, a vertical tortoise. Rex and Gus share glances. Gus looks like he feels this is going too far but won't act; he turns away.

'Gotta say, Crystal's five yer ol' looks pleasin',

quizzin' 'er thru me telescope. Leds ged on da pizz, Gus me mate, an see if we can, carn?'

Rex tries to get his leg working, to lift himself up so he can see over the lip of the window. Charge points at something through the glass.

'There's a few smart cunts need sortin' out real fast, right there.'

'Have you touched them?' Rex says before he knows it.

Charge stares at him a long moment before laughing. 'I can hit her if oi wanna. Bring back the biff!'

'What are you planning with Jenny Chan?' says Rex, only a slight treble in his voice.

'Yevgo wants me ta keep the kook happy so he can put the bite on her. "I've had vasectomy, yah. Ist good, yah?" But this is it, Rex. Right here. This is our chance, to start Australia with clean stock.'

'What on earth …?'

'You heard.'

Rex fixes Gus. 'You going along with this?'

Gus stares at his feet.

Charge laughs. '"We should be one people and remain one people without the admixture of other races." – know who said dat, doos ya? Alfred Deakin, our first prime minister.'

Charge walks to the door, nearly yanking it off its hinges in his haste to open it. He twists his neck muscles to glance back at Rex.

'The bitch is history.'

Charge lifts up his shirt. Tucked down his shorts: Rex's Colt Python.

Lying, sweating in bed, Rex tries all day to go back in time. He closes his eyes for the umpteenth attempt.

He is with Kerrie in her house in Seddon, the TV off, Buzz and Roger spread-eagled on the carpet near the heater.

'Oh, thank God,' he cries. Knowing there isn't much time, he gets straight to the point. 'Kerrie, I've told you not to take the job but I haven't told you why. I haven't told you what will happen if you do. Thank God I'm back!'

She stares at him. 'Back?' she laughs. 'We only just finished an exhaustive discussion – '

'Oh, good. We need – '

' – and you agreed a garage sale was better than trying to take all this with us to the outback.'

Rex goes cold.

There is a catch in her throat. 'What is it?'

He takes her in his arms and sobs. 'So you still took the job, after what I told you last time?'

'What last time? There is only now.'

He lets go of her, mumbling. 'This isn't a second chance. I hoped but ...'

'But what?'

'Oh God, Kerrie.'

'What!'

'We only ever had one shot.'

With his leg dressed, Rex grabs Yevgeny's arm.

'For the last time, will you help us?' he says between gritted teeth.

Yevgeny pushes his thick glasses up his Muppet-like nose with one, leather-gloved hand. 'My friend, I heerd you fond ofe tellink stories. I have story ofe my own, I theenk. First time patient squeal-ed under my knife, I knewt. I knewt as weel as anythink with total certainty. I sadist. There! I confess-ed it you.'

Rex slowly lets go his grip on Yevgeny's spongy arm, the armpit giving off odour in an almost visible cloud of spores from a grey mushroom.

'I don't vant I help you, Rex; I vant hurt you very bet.'

He presses his fingers in Rex's leg, imitating an America cheerleader. 'Give me an eight. Eight! Give me a nine. Nine! Give me a – '

Rex smacks Yevgeny on the side of the head. The man stumbles back against his trolley, scattering his implements, some falling on the floor. To Rex's surprise, Yevgeny sobs in histrionic, hiccupping fits.

Night. Seven days since he was shot. A month since climbing from his grave, the cellar. Jenny is reading to him from a book on agriculture.

'Jenny, let me get this right? You're pumping

water from the tableland with this truck's engine?'

She gives up and puts down the book. 'That's right.'

'You reckon we could get it unhooked and still drive it?'

Jenny stares at him like he's mad. 'Rex, this place is our last chance.'

'I'm planning on us coming back. But there's a gun at the Cressida. I calculate three shots. We need to get it and then we've got something to kill Charge with.'

She jumps off the chair. 'I thought you told me you weren't mad? Look, I don't like him either, the racist prick, but ...'

He takes her hand. His expression silences her.

'Jenny, we have to kill him because he's planning on killing *you*.'

Early next morning, Jenny shakes him awake. 'Charge and Yevgeny have gone to the dam. I've spoken to Crystal and Emmy. They're joining us. We've got an hour.'

Rex, supported by Crystal and Jenny (Emmy holding his busted left leg), surveys the truck. Someone smart has jacked it up off the floor and used a long fan belt to run the pump that's bringing up the water from the tableland. He unloops the fan belt, attaching a smaller one Jenny finds for him amongst the detritus of the shed. Then, helped down by the others, he lies on two overalls he's tied together. Crystal and Jenny grab the furthest arms of these and pull on them, dragging him under the truck. He looks up to see if he can loosen the brackets the truck is affixed by, then they can slide it off the rails and get it started. He calls for various tools and items – spanners, wrenches, grease, rags.

'We'll eat later, Emmy,' he says between orders.

'But, but, but, I *am* hungry. I'm just hungry. Just wanna have lunch now. Please can we have lunch now, Rex?'

'We have to move, sweetheart,' says Jenny.

'I don't wanna go out. We already goed out. I gived him a biscuit.'

Rex stops loosening a nut.

'Who?' asks Rex.

'Soldier.'

He rolls out painfully from under the truck.

'You saw her, Emmy?'

'By the hut.'

With Crystal and Emmy gone to fetch Soldier, Jenny helps Rex slide back under the truck, and stays lying on her side to watch and help when necessary.

'Crystal looked at me funny when I touched your knee, Rex.'

Rex doesn't answer as he works at the last nut, which is screwed on impossibly tight.

Jenny traces an oil leak on the concrete ground; car sweat. 'I know what that look of hers means. I guess we're none of us anybody's anymore.'

Rex takes her hand, stopping its circular motion. 'You're a beautiful girl, and if this were a beautiful world, you wouldn't look twice at me ...'

'I would.'

'No, you wouldn't. Because I could have stopped all this but I did nothing. I did nothing.'

'How?' she laughs.

'I mean, I could have stopped the outbreak.'

Her smile drops off her face like a feather attached to a lead weight.

There is a bang outside. She remains staring at him.

'Hey, you'd better let them in,' he tells her.

Rex hears three sets of steps. They must all be back.

'Nearly done.'

Not one of them answers.

Going cold, he quickly tries to scramble out from under the back of the truck. But before he can move, his feet are yanked from under him.

Blow after blow after blow as Charge beats him.

Rex is in the corridor of the military base. The same one he fell into and stayed several weeks. He is remembering the first time he mapped it out. Holding a taper, a flower spear he's taken from a grass tree, Soldier ever by his side, he comes across a door marked 'Strictly no admittance to unauthorised personnel.' An unreality swells as the moment recalls his youthful venture to his uncle's neighbouring property, where 'Weakness' was written in the doormat outside the house.

He must go in this time, in this place, but a great foreboding comes over him. Weakness.

He tries the lever with its complicated piston locking system. It unlatches from the doorjamb, side and top.

There is nothing now preventing him from entering, save that one word. Weakness. He pushes the door ajar, the corroded rubber seals squeaking. A stench rushes out to meet him. He takes an involuntary step back, Soldier also.

Free hand over his nose and forcing his courage, Rex enters. Sights are caught in the dim flame that make him gasp: animals starved to death in their cages. Mice, rats, cats and … dogs.

Dogs? This can only be one place: hers and Malcolm's laboratory.

'How could you, Kerrie?'

Soldier, one flank constantly brushing against his right leg, works her nose overtime. Her shackles raised, her tail pointed like a ballerina's under her body.

The stench.

His taper illuminates one last image of horror: a dead Chimp leaning against its cage, its hand through the bars like God's in Michelangelo's painting. But no human hand reaching back. He steps out of that room and locks a door on a memory he hadn't reopened till now. If there is one boon, it is very slight: this time he has overcome his weakness.

Charge stops kicking him.

He wakes to darkness. Jenny is crying. He feels a rib move and can only see out of one eye.

'Look who's here to see you, Rex.'

It is Soldier. She licks his cheek.

'Soldier! Soldier!'

His cries hurt his face.

In the clarity of the moment, he now sees what he should have done in the days and weeks after the outbreak: opened paddock gates to let out livestock, freed pigs and chickens from their factory prisons, filled in cattle grids. Given the world back. Not wasted time trying to find a gun. He would have died anyhow. Pitifully, perhaps, but not in one last selfish act. He should have busied himself giving the world back.

The blind is up. Outside, stars; stippled white on black.

He'd been thinking these flashbacks in time were a chance to reset things. Find a moment before Kerrie took her researches to the outback and make her stop.

But who would want to save such a world?

In the darkness of the room, he now sees he was wrong to let his resolve slip.

'How *could* you, Kerrie?'

The virus, the outbreak, the devastation and inevitable extinction wrought on the human species? He *did* want that to happen.

There is only one thing left that's real to him.

'Where's Soldier?' he murmurs to the empty room.

Rex lies bleeding on Yevgeny's operating table.

'Yous woulda got away, Rex. Got away if Gus 'adn't seen Crystal and her sprog puttin' Soldier on a leash to take inside. Got away with a gook. Then what? Mixed races like we got rats in this country, rabbits.'

Rex laughs blood. 'I know someone else wanted to wipe out introduced species. *There was an old woman who swallowed a fly …*'

'Is that fucken English? You toffy bastard.'

'*… I don't know why she swallowed the fly …*'

Soldier licks at his blood.

'*Perhaps she'll die.*'

Charge takes the Colt Python out of his shorts and

caresses Rex's swollen nose with the tip. 'Jenny Chan's gonna die, that's who.'

Rex stops laughing with a start. 'What does it matter?' he screams, the fissure in his top lip reopening.

Charge steps back.

'Yeah, steady goes it, Charge,' adds Gus.

Charge stares at him.

Rex lifts himself up on a shoulder, blood trickling from his mouth. 'What on earth does it matter? Who cares if races mix? Look at Soldier. She's a bitser. I mean, there's blue heeler in her, bit of kelpie too. Goodness knows what else; she isn't a pure breed. But I still love her: she's still a great dog.'

Charge puts the Colt down his shorts and picks at the dirt under his fingernails.

'You're right.'

They stare at him.

'Phew,' mutters Gus. 'You had me goin' there, Charge me mate.'

Rex breathes out slowly, the pain in his chest easing.

'Yous perfectly right.'

'Thank God,' Rex mutters under his breath.

'Yous right she isn't a pure breed. She's the first to go.'

Charge grabs her by the neck, the Colt Python retrieved once more and in his other hand.

'Please! Please don't touch my dog. Please, man,

don't touch her!'

Soldier whimpers and tries to twist in his hand.

'Come on, Charge,' pleads Gus, 'you've proved your point.'

'Please, man, not my dog!'

'Urrr, urrr.'

Rex tries to move but his every joint sings with pain.

'*Please!*'

'Look at yous, ya pissweak cunt. Squalling over a fucken dog. If there was some cunt wid a gun to me head, you'd be tellin' 'im, pull the trigger. And I'm your fucken brother, bud. We're the same species, mate. Same fucken race!'

Rex, hand out: 'Hey, mate, not my dog. Please. Please!'

'You beggin', that just makes me wanna do it more. Like all me pissweak mates. Talk, talk. Those guys professed to be pretty tough and bogun. But make a comment 'bout Jews and post a bit of rape porn and they'd go to water.'

Soldier twists and yelps in his hand.

'Please, man, she's my best friend. Please don't hurt my dog.'

He drags her outside. She peers back imploringly as the door shuts. And shoots. The last shot.

'Oh God, oh God!'

Rex twists the blood-spattered sheet in his hand.

'Oh God, oh God, where are you? Soldier, baby,

Soldier.'

'Too far,' mutters Gus. 'He's taken it too far.'

Rex sobs. Gus puts a hand on his shoulder. Rex throws it off, digging his hand into the sheet, the sheet he wishes was Soldier's ruff.

'Oh God.'

He doesn't get to go back in time and make everything right, and he doesn't get to keep Soldier.

'I'm sorry, Soldier ...'

Charge walks back in, alone.

Rex twists the sheet in a knot till the blood seeps out through his fingers. He stares at Charge with the most focused rage he's known. He is back to square one: he just wants one shot.

CHAPTER SIX

Rex asks himself, what happened? Where did the time go? When you're young, life seems so long. At age ten, thinking back to when you were five is half a lifetime ago! But as you grow into your teens, twenties, thirties and beyond, each year seems to rush past with ever increasing speed, leaving more dreams unrealised, longer lists of things undone, things you're never likely to get done. At such moments, it is like Rex has nearly suffered death and seen his life flash past, with all its false starts, wrong paths, alternating torrents/dearths of feeling.

At other moments, what most gladdens him is that there will be no one to build on anything, to improve or corrupt what went before. No one to put in extensions, rejig recipes, revamp kitchens or any of the other various activities we do to certify we're alive. No, at those times, he just wants a general decay, an unravelling of our world to its baser, more honest, constituents.

No one has bothered to raise the blind and let in the sunlight that frames it. He is in too much pain to get up and do it himself. It takes him a while to notice Jenny is watching him from the fifties chair, face impassive.

'You could have stopped all this?'

He tells her the story.

She gets up and walks out.

Rex stares at the shadowed ceiling and screams with pain and grief. 'Help me!'

He is with Kerrie six weeks after they met, all the anxiousness and stress of meeting nearly dwindled, but still the air of frisson, the excitement. Before the miasmal rot.

They're standing on the beach near Rye, amongst a graveyard of driftwood skeletons lazily half-buried in the sand. He imagines how the scene must figure from the sky. The intersection of surf and beach: the cross-sectioned growth rings of some colossal tree. And there, a tiny knot, him and Kerrie.

'Remember this moment,' he says to Kerrie. 'This was the best we ever were.'

She looks at him funny. '*Were*? This is another dream, isn't it? An alternate universe?'

A pair of seagulls sea-saw on the salt wind.

'Why couldn't you have talked to me like this in life, Rex?'

He beams, affixing her dark green eyes. 'You are here with me in my dreams then?'

'Only in *my* dreams.' Her face comes over pale with a troubling thought. 'Or *are* they yours?'

'I guess it doesn't much matter,' he laughs.

So many moments lost in time. So many feelings, expressions. But why does the world forget? A necessary amnesia? What matters if it doesn't last?'

They gaze upon the corrugated water.

It was that moment when you say, Come into my life. Forever never lasts. Ever.

'Oi shoulda gived ya that gun,' whispers Crystal in the darkness of his room, only her lighter illuminating them with its flickering.

Rex painfully lifts himself to lean against the iron headrest, and nods.

'Oi didna want you ta 'ave an out now, did oi?'

Rex tries to turn away from her, pain stabbing his side. She leans over him and takes his puffy face in her hands. 'Live,' she sobs. 'Tell me you wanna live. Please. Be heaps easier.'

Rex can only look down to avoid her hazel-eyed gaze. Crystal leans in closer, lips pursed. That's the last thing he wants right now. But it is only to whisper to him.

'Oi needs ya, baby. Emmy needs ya. Yous 'ave ta

protect us in 'ere, orright?'

He plays with a yellow plastic earring she must have found, half hidden in her blonde/auburn hair. She quickly draws away, glancing at the door.

'What about the other gun, the Beretta that soldier shot himself with? Did you go back for it?' he asks.

She shakes her head. A good thing, probably. Charge obviously took Rex's Colt off her. If she'd had the Beretta, he'd now still be armed, with three shots.

'I'm sorry, orright. She was a rool good dog. Emmy's not stopped crying 'bout it. They was rool good togeva.'

Rex stiffens. Emmy, as defenceless in her own way as Soldier, as innocent of this world they'd made as her … he's still responsible. If he'd let Soldier get hurt, he couldn't let Emmy.

Rex examines his father smoking. 'Mum died of cancer – why would you still smoke?'

His father studies the cigarette a long time. 'How do you want your afterlife, son? Smoking or non-smoking!'

Uncharacteristically, his father guffaws.

In the morning, Gus wheels Rex out to the river. They see a red and white steamship bogged in the shallows, looking like a toy, its paddles a wind-up mechanism. A rook sits on its sloping stern, mugging detachment. On the far bank, a herd of cattle wade in the mud, wagging their bottom jaws from left to right. Trunks lean out over the water, their mayonnaise bellies alive with slithering serpents of light.

Rex inhales deeply the fragrance of water that's living, that carries life, mud and meaning, mixed with the unselfish chatter of life. It's a beautiful day.

Gus hovers at his shoulder. Rex broaches the subject Gus can't.

'He doesn't know what he's doing, does he?'

Instant agreement: 'No, he fucking well does not. He's a mad bastard, all right. The way he's using up our resources on his half-cocked schemes, we'll be fucked in a month.'

Rex looks at the ground, at the trident-footprint of birds who've edged out to the water, who've shallow-skimmed their throats full, who've fluffed their wings with spray, whose bodies were briefly adorned with droplets as regal as any ceremonial garb before they discarded them with a shake and launched, naked, into the air.

'You told me once you cut your livestock's throats yourself,' says Rex, and leaves it at that.

Gus moves out behind him, leaning a hand on the bole of a lacerated trunk, kicking at the water with his Blundstones. His free hand scratches the white bristles on his red cheek.

'Fuck it, man, I talk to them. I talk to them as I do it. Think *he's* gonna let me get an arm round his neck while I coo in his ear?

Clouds, like pillows, smother the sun; the cool makes Rex shiver.

'I buried her for ya. Only right.'

Rex can't suppress a moan. He waits till he can trust his throat again before asking, 'Has he mentioned Jenny lately?'

'No. But that's no reason to relax. Crystal told me every three weeks, he goes troppo. Each time it's worse than the last. You know the last. We've got five days left to act.'

Rex pulls the blanket round him. The cold is creeping in with the night, the insects also heralding the day's demise with their increased chirping. A cicada lands on his chest, a beautiful emerald green brooch.

Gus stiffens and grabs the wheelchair, saying loudly, 'Well, can't be here all day. Some of us have got work to do.'

Rex likewise stiffens. Gus wheels Rex back. How much, if anything, did Charge overhear?

Light fills the room like a rapidly expanding bubble, enveloping him without popping. Startled awake, Rex lifts himself painfully to a sitting position, still squinting, his fingers held up, scissoring the light.

'Who ... who is it?'

Rex makes out Charge holding a lantern, the kerosene smell sickening. 'Oh God, no.'

He pushes himself against the iron bed-rest, his caged heart flapping against his ribs. Charge strolls in, pulling up at the foot of the bed.

'Oi, what ya getting like dat for? Bin thinking. We's shud be mates, bud. Got off on the wrong foot, didn't we? Can't av you plottin' now. Time I rewarded yas.'

Rex blinks.

'Agreed, brus?'

Rex quickly nods.

'Yous don't hafta act scared wid me, mate. You'll just shit me, doin' that.'

Rex forces nonchalance, playing with the button on his pyjama top.

'I mean, we's the same stock. Most Anglo here, right? Gus fucken looks like a skinned pig. Yevgo has neutered his genes wid drink, right? An yous know how I feel 'bout the kook. Wot oi'm getting at, bro, it's up to us, innit?'

Rex nods slowly when he realises Charge is waiting for his response. Charge slaps his shank of a thigh with a laugh and leaves the room. Rex shivers queasily. He can't get going, can't move. Is Charge coming back? What's his game? That leering look he gave him when he left …? Oh God, oh God, what will he do, what *can* he do? He can't move. He can't defend himself. The door flies open, Rex making a noise he's never issued before; almost a squeak.

Anger flames up with the fear: how this monster has unmanned him …

Charge is with Crystal, arm hanging loose round her neck. Emmy is hugging Crystal's leg. Crystal gets out a twisted smile.

'Sorry 'bout the sprog,' laughs Charge. 'Insists, I hear. Tell it to turn to the wall, ha ha. 'Ere, Crystal's yours. Your kids are moi kids, right? Eh, what's that dribblin' for?'

Charge leaves, laughing. Crystal and Emmy hug Rex, joining him in his grief. He winces with his broken ribs.

'Eh, gentle, Em,' says Crystal.

Rex catches a glimpse of Jenny as he waves Crystal and Emmy off from his room in the morning.

The days stretch out; two weeks pass. Charge is jovial, but there is always that terrifying undercurrent of uncertainty. The able adults go about their various activities during the day. Rex, in his incapacitated state, becomes a playmate for Emmy. Charge seems to have no interest in her except to at times make her cry over some imagined failure of manners – dinners, usually, the one meal they all share. These 'lessons' are infrequent and half-hearted as though it were more to do with reminding Rex of her paternity.

When Rex or Crystal intercedes, Charge embarks on endless diatribes about how they are making her weak and spoilt. Emmy bears all with an uncanny silence for a five-year-old. It seems to go easier *not* pleading on Emmy's behalf and that makes hers and their defeat even greater, even more sharply humiliating.

'Why did you go out with him?' Rex asks Crystal in a rare moment they have alone. She's in his room, knowing Charge and Gus are searching the nearest property for supplies.

'Oi felt sorry for 'im, didn't oi?'

For Rex, this doesn't compute. Crystal notes his sceptical frown and simpers.

'Plus he's fucken hot, eh.'

Rex half concedes: 'Till he opens his mouth, maybe.'

Crystal seems strangely pleased by his response and laughs before lightly slapping him on the shoulder.

'Yous jealous!'

'Not at all,' mumbles Rex, biting on the words.

She gives him a mooing look. 'Hey, it's orright. Yous kind of hot, too.'

She pulls his cheek till he can't help but grin. She kisses him, reaching under the blankets. He gently stops her. 'I'm still sore.'

She shrugs. 'Oi'm not.'

Laughing himself finally, he takes her in his arms.

In the dappled shade of the shed, with its Braille

corrugated iron, Charge sits Rex down and talks to him at length – though he doesn't use these words, nothing like them – of how he has rid Rex of 'extraneous loyalties'. All Rex can think about is how the spotted light on Charge's face makes the man look like he's wearing a bridal veil. It's an image so incongruous a smile distorts Rex's mouth.

'Why yas laughin'? Oi'm pourin' me heart out to yas.'

Charge's words fall out with a disjointed horror. Were diatribes like this the reason Crystal felt sorry for him? Seems Charge has more than enough sympathy for himself.

Before long, Rex is startled to see the man crying.

'Yous mean. Yous all so mean and suspicious 'bout me. What av *I* done? Me, the best of all of yas!'

He leans forward. Rex realises what that means: he must hug this man.

'Oi had ta kill ya dog, mate. Ya see that, don't yas?'

It is all Rex can do not to throw up over Charge's shoulder like a burped baby.

Rex hobbles to the vegetable garden and spies Jenny, tying tomato bushes to stakes. She stops and falls to her knees in the dirt, holding one of the tomatoes close to her cheek. The tomato's plump and juicy, which makes Rex think of what it's been nourished with: the uncontaminated water pumped from the tableland. His eyes skip from it to Jenny's troubled face.

'What is it?' he asks.

She turns to look up at him.

'There's something that scares me to death about this. Steaming the water should get rid of the virus.'

She stands, letting go of the tomato. Rex starts on another tack. Impatient, she grabs his collar.

'Steaming even gets rid of *radiation* in water.'

The seeming impossibility of getting the virus out of water has bothered Rex, too, though he didn't know steaming even gets rid of radiation. 'Yes ... well ...'

Her face contorting with anger, she shakes him. 'What did your girlfriend do, Rex? Fuck with physics?'

Jenny pushes past him, a cry beginning in her throat. It's the first time he's heard her swear.

Well, Kerrie didn't mess with physics. But perhaps Gary did.

Three weeks clocked up at this nightmare commune, and things aren't going well in terms of their prospects. Jenny and Gus take care of the vegetables, but they are grown outside and there is no protection for when it rains. It rains even in the desert. When it does, that contaminated rainwater will seep down to the tableland and spoil their untarnished supply. They need to dredge up as much unspoilt water as they can now, find more containers to stockpile it. They must create a closed environment for their vegetables, roof their little patch, as if they were now aliens to their own world, as welcome as visitants to the inhospitable moon. It is difficult to raise these matters rationally with Charge. He takes it either as a critique of his self-appointed leadership, or an ambition to undermine him. Their small excursions into his policy don't yet make him explode but they lead him to the brink, and they must draw back. Gus pushes most gently, with jokes and asides. Rex will say something now and then but his droopy left eyelid, permanent limp from a kick where he was shot and a caved left cheekbone more often than not hold him in silence.

Over one of their 'family' dinners, Jenny watches Rex sulkily. She's confided that their last bottle of methylated spirits has gone, and wants him to mention it. Rex knows who the culprit is: Yevgeny. However, Yevgeny isn't the sole recipient of its contents and this is what mutes Rex: he's seen and heard Gus and Charge also partaking of the Russian's home brew.

Charge is in one of his proselytising moods. During the most rabid bits, he makes mention of 'the kooks' that want 'our land.'

Rex avoids Jenny's eyes. But then the insanity all gets too much.

'Hey!' he blurts out despite his weakness.

Charge stops talking and stares at him.

'Hey …' says Rex, more softly, already backtracking. 'I've got a headache, that's all. You're a pretty fast talker, mate.'

The others watch Charge to see what he'll do. Charge spits out the husk of a nut he's been chewing on.

'A bit slow, are ya, brus? Give your wee little head a rest. Oi'm done.'

He's dreaming he's a teddy bear that Crystal is knitting.

Jenny is next to him in the dark.

'I was a long-distance runner,' she says.

He tries to open his eyes. But no one has thought to give him eyes yet.

'I'll get to this dead soldier and get the Beretta.'

He finds buttons for eyes and looks at her. 'I don't …' he mumbles, still waking up. 'I mean, he hasn't mentioned you directly for a few days … You're probably safe for the – '

'Just tell me how to get there.'

'Hey,' he calls out before she slips through the door. 'You really believe we keep living over our lives till we get them right?'

She manages a quarter smile. 'Yes, you've still got centuries to redeem yourself.'

She shuts the door behind her.

Rex waits all day for Jenny to return. Emmy intuits

how distracted he is and gets petulant with him. Charge doesn't notice Jenny's gone till everyone's stopped work for the day. The evening meal, as served by Yevgeny, is a long one. No one mentions her absence. Rex feels Charge's eyes shift from one of them to the next. Rex can't eat.

Yevgeny produces an old-fashioned watch from his pocket that needs to be wound. How the numerical time of day has ceased to matter to Rex. Yevgeny leaves and returns with a rare desert he's concocted.

In resuming his seat, Yevgeny totters and smashes into the table. A smart rebuke would usually be forthcoming, but Charge is silent.

After a long silence, Yevgeny ogles Rex's untouched soup and stewed pear desert.

'So-o-o, Rex, ist it true? Once you havt tasted human flesh, you can't go back, dah!'

Rex stumbles outside, scanning the steely blue night for a shape looming into focus. Still she doesn't come. The canopy of the pepper tree chirps and beeps. He looks up to see tattered black umbrellas hanging from its branches; a flock of fruit bats.

What can he do? Is she hurt? Did Charge follow her?

Rex hears the door open behind him. The bats fly off in silence, all black muscle and sinew. Charge has come outside to join Rex, propping open the screen door with his bulk. Again, there is no rebuke.

Rex is in bed, his pillow feeling like a chopping block. No Crystal, no Emmy tonight. Is Charge punishing him? Did Charge know of his and Jenny's plan to retrieve the gun? And if so, how did he get that information? From Crystal …? Not likely.

Or … from Jenny, before he must've …

But if Charge knows, then why no reprisal? When Rex tried to take the truck and leave with the girls, Charge's punishment was swift and brutal. This time, the lack of response has an air of chess about it; a considered calculation between moves.

He must find out first thing in the morning if Gus noticed Charge leaving during the day. But by then that will be a whole day and night for Jenny in who knows what circumstances.

He gets off to sleep in the wee hours of the morn, but it is a troubled slumber. Unusually, his mind seeks for a religious understanding of these events, hailing different creeds, each one to him crumbling monuments of imagination's imagining. It is with feeble mastery that he reins in the terror of a night spent groping after doubt. Something out of grasp – possibly even an answer of sorts – evades him. He tries harder, but when even deep communing fails to make the unseen seen, what can he do? What is it Kerrie's ghost said to him …? 'I can't let go of you, Rex. I can't let go and move on.' Oh Kerrie, he cries –

a magnet has sent his heart's compass spinning.

He wakes to find it is night still. The stars that gem the sky are like the many eyes of some monstrous spider, its attitude to his predicament total indifference. He isn't even nourishing enough to eat.

He pulls the blanket over his head, a child again, and quickly makes lists, lists of the memories he feels will be lost to him before he is even dead.

Oh, such times! Like when your laughter has an echo: friends. Brushing against that someone who'll become that one: a pretty, kiss-exacting girl. Snorkling with mates at twenty-three, and seeing a Box Jellyfish – disembodied brain and spinal cord, turquoise in a sea of dreams. The merest caress of its ganglia, and ...

No, not that memory of pain. He must seek others. Recent ones. The land! Yes, the land he has since the crises felt a privileged custodian of rather than rightful heir to. The feelings, the percipient sensations he's had, the awareness of presences! Ancient ghosts to whom we would have nothing to say. And oh, their haunts! A cool grotto, with a portcullis of dripping water feebly barring the way to its wet innards. Cool, dank caves with groined arches of quartzite. The merest world of insects and lizards, that we giants are too clumsy to appreciate.

Rex feels he could make these lists all day, of what he has seen and sees. He never before wondered how a ghost might occupy itself; perhaps this is how:

itemising memories missed, in both senses of that susurrus word.

His father, stuck in that frieze of the curiously empty café courtyard: 'Don't you think this might be limbo? That life was before this, a walled garden we've locked ourselves out of? After all, what is the definition of hell, Rex? To suffer perpetual thirst.'

Rex's father was of that annoying species of Christian who don't even countenance the idea that anyone could be genuinely atheist. Thus their arguments always proceed from an assumption that everyone is at least agnostic at heart.

'So this is hell, right?' Rex humours him.

His father ashes into his empty can of bourbon and dry. 'Heaven is a place on Earth. We just have to make that true.'

He's not sure how he really feels about this, about any of this, about how to feel while he does feel.

Morning finally comes to boil.

Still the explosion arising from Jenny Chan's disappearance doesn't come, despite many days' simmering. When Charge does finally broach the topic, he comes instead to boast that she'd saved himself the job. Rex incubates a sickness. Is Charge lying when he implies he has had nothing to do with her absence? If he isn't, that still begs the question: what happened to her?

'I dunno,' says Gus by the river, Rex walking this time with the aid of a makeshift crutch. 'I dunno if he knows. But I reckon he heard our conversation the other day.'

Rex presses. 'Did you look for her?'

Gus stops walking, the pillared trees widely spaced enough for them to know this time they're alone.

'Mate, I went as far as I could, but that mongrel watches me all day like he watches everyone else.'

Gus hurries back to their dwellings. Rex hops after him.

Over dinner, Charge catches Rex sizing him up. Charge merely beams.

In his room, alone again for the night, Rex gets down on the floor and does his push-ups, his busted foot hitched behind the good one. In the day, he must feign greater disability. He will be ready. This time he'll be ready.

It's halfway through February. Two weeks at this place. Nearly ten weeks since Kerrie's death. Two and a half months since the outbreak.

The door flies open, hitting the wall and waking Rex in an instant. He squints in the full daylight – he's slept in. Charge enters wearing only a towel round his waist, his bronze body glistening from a bucket shower. That familiar feeling of nausea that hijacks Rex's gut on sight of Charge returns. He wonders if he can feign sleep but knows he stiffened on Charge entering.

Charge saunters to the window, where his body is lit frontally, accentuating his sculptured muscles. He stands with weight slightly back, one hand on the sill, the other held slightly out to the side. There is something unambiguous of a pose in it, a challenge, an exhibition of seamless masculinity in contrast to Rex's now crumpled self. It is like he stands as the prized pedigree mastiff, bred for brutality and force, next to the stray mongrel, kicked down, cowering, flea-bitten and marked.

Does Charge know about Rex's muscle-building exercises? Is this his riposte? *Look at me, then at your scrawny self.* The nerve!

For a man usually so talkative, this silence is perhaps Charge's greatest and most unnerving display of superiority since the initial thrashing he gave Rex. It occurs to Rex now that Charge would not have considered that beating a loss of control in his own mind, but a very calculated display to ensure continuity and cohesion of their 'pack'.

Rex, clothed and under a blanket, should feel the less exposed next to this near-nakedness, but the opposite is true: prostrate to this preening sturdiness, this upright force, this physically untarnished tank, he is unmade once more and feels that anger and shame borne by the abused.

Under Charge's right collarbone, the Australian flag tattooed in green and gold, the colours sickly against the skin. Across his planed shoulders, something written in elaborately old English text, the angle too oblique to read. Around his arms, interlacing Celtic thorns. His body maps a hotchpotch of borrowed cultures and beliefs, which to Charge plainly represent a proud display of European ancestry.

Rex feels an excruciating pain: should he speak? Pretend still to be asleep even though he knows Charge is aware he's watching him; desires this as his boast? Where will it go, how will the paused moment bump into play? When the suspension seems too great, Charge deliberately stretches his other leg, and the fold in the towel comes achingly apart. It slides away down his legs to expose his hanging muscle and weighty balls. There is almost no hair on his body except for a quiff of gold above his cock.

Jarring as physical force, a thought occurs to Rex as to the reason for this visit. He arches in the bed in fear, pulling the blanket tightly to him. Oh God, no, no, no. Please no, not that.

Charge's lip upwardly curves. 'We's mates, Rex. Oi feel we've become rool good mates, us. Our first little fight, when I found out you was screwin' Crystal and all … Well, that doesn't bother me now I know we's sharing her. Makes us closer.'

Rex moves his eyes to the red door, then back.

'Emmy's gonna make a hot girl, isn't she? Give her fathers grief. There won't be blokes round fer her. Guess it's got to be us, right? She'll be six soon. That's not too young to school her. Since yer me brother, Rex, I'm gonna give yas first dibs.'

Rex's eye drops down to Charge's groin: his cock has swollen. Charge takes it in hand.

'Yeah, rool sexy she'll … hnr … turn … agh … out.'

Heaving to a climax, Charge leaves, not bothering to wipe up the mess or pick up the towel. Rex limps to the window and looks at what Charge was looking at: Crystal is crouched down, weeding round the greens of the carrots; but behind her, half concealed, is Emmy, gathering small clods of clay in a pile with a little trowel, her face still fresh and welcoming and hopeful.

He can't wait another day.

Rex peeps out the hospice front door. Gus is walking to the tank, to fill buckets. Charge is in the tractor shed, back turned, ferreting among boxes. Rex skips over to Gus, shushing him and hurrying him behind the concrete tank, out of sight of Charge.

'Hey, you're moving a lot better now, aren't – '

'Gus, keep him busy. Don't let him drop in on me today.'

'Eh? How?' asks Gus.

'I don't fucking care. Just do it.'

Rex peeps round the curved wall of the tank to see Charge crouched down now, looking under the shed bench. Rex glances across to the edge of the forest, a twenty-metre run.

'Hey, Rex, before you go, I've been thinking.'

Rex stares at him.

'You know, them Aborigines might've known a thing or two after all. That story of theirs, 'bout Tiddalik – know that one?'

'No. Gus, I need you to – '

'Now just shut up and listen a minute. I think they were onta somethin'. This Tiddalik frog, right, he gets this unquenchable thirst, and goes about slurpin' up all the fresh water till it's all gone, see. Now where does that leave everyone else? Fuckin' parched, that's where. But this wise wombat gets this eel fellow to tie himself in knots and that makes Tiddalik laugh up all the water. Now come on, you must've fuckin' been taught it at school. What kinda prissy school you went to anyway?'

'Yeah, I went to a private school.'

'It's written all over you. There's a frog like that, you know. A real one. Central Australia somewhere. (If there are any frogs left, that is.) During the rainy season, gets its eatin' and rootin' done, then soaks up all the water and buries itself in the earth during the dry season. To avoid desiccation. There's a big word for you – you should know what that means.'

Rex grabs Gus' shoulders. 'Keep him busy. Please.'

'Yeah, yeah. But I think I've worked it out.'

'Worked what out?'

'This. All this. What's happening.'

Rex pats him on the shoulder; Gus isn't a bad bloke. 'Tell me when I get back, all right?'

'Sure. Be off with ya.'

Rex makes a lopsided run for it, reaching the tree line. He hides behind a wide trunk, third row in, and glances back. Gus turns away and intercepts Charge walking towards the hospice. A few words and Gus redirects Charge to the garden.

On the way, Rex passes a fitted-out bus with noise coming from within. He looks in the window to see Yevgeny hunched over beacons and solutions. He's found the man's distillery.

Rex hurries on, coming out the other side of the wood and into the open desert. He looks to the sun. He calculates he's got five hours. Two there, two back? That leaves one for leeway. He doesn't have his old mobility, though ... They have dinner at six, the time Charge will notice he's missing if he hasn't already by then. No time to dawdle.

She's dead. He can't see any sign of how she died. No obvious cause, but its hard with her body bloated and black and aromatic with flies. She's tried to write something with pebbles and sticks. S-N-A? He can't read the last letter. One of the twigs is still in her hand, unplaced. A laugh explodes unchecked from his lips. He does an uncoordinated dance in the dust, his left foot stinging, swivelling back to the scene in a drunken pirouette. He puts a grimy hand in his mouth to stop his obscene, irreverent chortling. Just what *isn't* wrong with him? But the scene smacks so absurdly of an Agatha Christie whodunit. And there must be moments to laugh amid all this horror, mustn't there? Poor Jenny.

He searches for a stick on the fragmented ground strong enough to lever her over, but eventually settles for hands; she doesn't deserve to be prodded. Her white teeth stand out in her tarnished face like cheap prop fangs from a joke shop. Indignity in death. Her hair is still beautiful. He can't find the gun on her. Strangely, she's ripped off her left sleeve to tie round her right thigh. Why?

Not able to bury her in the baked ground – who will visit the grave anyway? – Rex continues on.

He tries to finish the word as he walks, turning the letters over in his mind. S-N-A ...? SNAP? An acronym? Sensitive New Age Guy? Hardly.

Her dead and dried face keeps superimposing itself over her alive face, over her smiling countenance. Which is the more real? What meaning existence, if the latter?

He walks past the Cressida, coming across the carnage of his shootout with Ross and Thor, a couple of minutes later. Thor doesn't seem to be present. Did he survive? Not likely, with the hole in his head Rex put there. Ross is lying where he shot himself. No Beretta, though …? Rex looks over the embankment. Thor, in parts. Dragged there by dingoes, wild dogs? Thor doesn't have the handgun on him, either. Weird? It wasn't on Jenny.

Fear winds him.

Frantically, he lopes back to the Cressida, worried that perhaps Charge killed Jenny despite protestations of innocence, that he's had the Beretta since her disappearance, that he'll be waiting for Rex at the hospice with three shots.

He sees the Beretta, on the dashboard of the Cressida, and opens the door. S-N-A …? He leans in. Perhaps it was more than four letters? Dark stain on the seat – must be his blood. He reaches forward. Is that last letter she half wrote a K? His hand gropes in the pellets of smashed windscreen and odd black shapes. SNAK? And if the word is five letters? He completes the word, and pulls his hand back just in time as the snake strikes.

Falling on his backside in the dust, Rex scrambles backwards. It plops off the seat and onto the ground, a tiger snake, with its beaded coat, yellow and brown. He gropes for a branch, flicks it in the middle. It lands, a figure-eight, before uncoiling infinity to come at him again, its head and neck surfing on air. He gets to his feet, before backtracking then jumps on the boot, only to stare at scalped Medusa; the snake's freshly hatched young.

Grey metal winks at him in the sun. The Beretta is in the midst of the serpents. Without a moment's pause, he snatches it up. Incredibly, he is unbitten and rolls off the bonnet and onto his feet, which are already running. When he is sure the parent snake isn't pursuing, he falls to the ground.

'Thank you, Jenny. Thank you …'

He's got back her smiling face, and blanked out that other.

Rex examines the gun as he walks. As he calculated, it has three shots. Emmy, Crystal, himself. But as for what he might need on Charge …?

He wished he'd fetched his sword from under the half-smashed rear windscreen, but hadn't risked it.

Rex looks up and, what he sees makes him stop. Is it six already? Has he miscalculated? Dark clouds smudge the sky; the underside of snails as seen through glass. A cymbal crash of thunder. A wind whips up. Rain falls, slanting in cut-along-the-lines, the water as foreign to the ground as in a tomb. The snails multiply, their shadows darkening the ground. Ticks of lightning take photos of the tonsured hills, reminding Rex of the vastness of the world, even in comparison to human ego. The tears of rain become sobs.

The smell of baked earth livens with the wet,

filling Rex's nostrils. His hair, shirt and trousers are plastered to his body, becoming a skin a couple of sizes too large with their folds and creases.

He's not really sure how to feel about it all. *Water, water everywhere nor any drop to drink.* He is parched Tantalus made to stand amid the sweet-tasting river.

Mini-torrents vein the ground, becoming rills and runnels, while mini-cliffs of sand break away, joining the mustard yellow flow of sand; a Lilliputian Grand Canyon in minutes.

How this land will bloom. He looks down at his feet, at the water already up to his ankles. How every pore in the earth must be opening up to receive this gift, sinking down, down to … the tableland! … The water will get in the tableland, their last uncontaminated supply! Will the others drink it? He makes sure to keep his own mouth shut as it streams down his face. Squinting through the rain, he makes out the compound still a good kilometre off.

He limps briskly through the acupuncture rain, his splashing forming musketeer boots at his ankles. Several rents open in the clouds, letting through skeins of light. The deluge slackens; great plops of rain are now distinguishable from each other on his head and shoulders.

He slows his pace, for there, on the outskirts of their habitat, his back to him, stands a man in a long coat, statuesque. From the shape, it can only be Gus.

Rex calls.

A couple of fingers on Gus' right hand spasm and twitch, a movement then copied in his left, as if he were warming up to conduct an orchestra.

There is something uncharacteristically abstruse in the gesture for Gus. Rex slows, his boots boats, beaching on the mud. Even amid the earth's popping and gulping, his plashing seemed very loud.

'Gus …?' he whispers. Gus turns and Rex almost gets water in his mouth from screaming. That face …

He staggers backwards, overbalancing, crashing into the mud. He lurches forward, getting to his hands and knees. Between his legs, he sees Gus running in an epileptic fury straight at him.

He hasn't time to retrieve his gun and fire.

With his left hand yanking his left foot forward, Rex half runs, half skips, keeping the closest building of their habitat in sight.

He glances over his right shoulder; he won't make it. Gus is bearing down on him like a Catherine Wheel.

A barbed wire fence looms. Rex throws his body sideways over it, using his right hand as a vault, getting a scratch and two iron bites as his reward. He falls heavily in the mud and water.

Gus ploughs into the wire, his mouth snapping, squid-like, centimetres from Rex's face, the hexagonal wire weave cutting into the man's face as

235

a macabre robber's stocking.

The one good eye in that face expresses nothing but insatiable, cannibalistic hunger.

Get up.

Rex, get up.

The pain is back in his body, the adrenalin only having briefly driven it out. He uses his hands as stirrups to lift his bad leg to standing position, and lumbers jerkily to the main building.

Having built to a trot again, he pushes his way through the falling beads of water, like so many of those plastic slatted entrances on shopfronts to keep out flies, but one hanging behind the other hanging behind the other. A dream-like slowness of doors.

A screaming behind him, furious. Allowing a quick look, Rex sees that Gus has broken free and is bearing down on him again, covered in a fear-inspiring war paint of mud and blood.

Rex throws himself at the door, which opens before he collides with it.

All he can make out for a long moment is the sound of thunderous crashing, which reminds him of when his dogs would bash on the back door to get in after he'd sent them out in the morning. But then Charge's voice comes over it.

'Shee-it, looksh what the cat brought in!'

Charge slurs his words some more, but all he says is garbage. Drunk? On Yevgeny's toxic mix? Had Gus been drunk too? Is that how this happened? Rex fumbles in his wet clothes for the gun. (Will it still work?).

He quickly stands to better protect himself from an assault. He hears the sound of what he thinks is the first strike but realises it is Gus ramming the door, splintering the glass.

They're in the enclosed veranda running one side of the hospice.

To Rex's surprise, Charge giggles.

'Hee hee, heesh fucken hammered, brus.'

'What?' asks Rex, horrified, finding the gun at last in his pocket.

'Oi, here he comes ag'in!'

Charge giggles as Gus rams the door, the square of glass falling out and the wood splintering down the middle.

Rex backs into the wall, drawing the gun. Charge looks at its barrel a second before grinning.

'Do it. I want you to, brus.'

Another voice behind him. He looks through the window into the industrial kitchen. Yevgeny, drunk too? Holding something in his hands ... A lighter? For the first time, Rex notes the strong smell of gas. There are compressed cylinders lined up on the aluminium bench.

The man's quoting scripture.

'... who led you through that great and terrible wilderness, in which were fiery serpents and scorpions and thirsty land where there was no water; who brought water for you out of the flinty rock; who …'

Another thud from Gus. Charge giggles. Yevgeny notices Rex and eyeballs him.

'I werk it out, my friend. We in hell. But if we in hell, wheret the fire? I make that now.'

Yevgeny flicks the lighter.

Rex throws himself on the ground, pulling his coat over his head, as the place erupts in a fireball.

He thinks about the days, the days that have gone. Those days when we're on the cusp of adulthood, when we think anything is possible and have energy and faith to almost make that 'anything' happen; the days when our lives could have turned out differently, when we could still have made the right choices, taken the best path. When we were still green.

All the people we pass by, all the lives we could have had; when we felt we belonged in the world, and longed to find that place of belonging; when we believed it existed; when the fact of just being alive, the lottery of it, was a miracle in itself, and reason enough for gratitude; that strange feeling that the fact that I am me and you are you is wonderful and beautiful and memorable. That feeling, where did it go? When we wanted to live remarkably, not just get by with as little drama as possible.

He thinks about Jenny's Buddhist beliefs that she imparted to him. The anxiety of Dukkha originates from a 'thirst', which can be seen as a combination of desire, craving and greed. The thirst that is at the core of even the most sated life.

Rex comes to. Embers settle round him as black snow. A dusting of glass silvers his body. The wall next to him, double-brick, is cracked. He feels for wounds. None. His wet clothes – completely dry now – must have saved him from catching alight. Getting to a sitting position, he sees a black, smoking shape. Charge, kneeling, with several fingers of his left hand blown off and his left ear hanging upside down like a loose part on a toy, stares back from boiled egg eyes. There is a whole right arm in his lap but Charge still has his right arm; it must be Yevgeny's. Holding the man's stare, for the first time Rex recognises the look in Charge that Crystal found pitiful.

Apart from the whoosh of the fire beginning to take hold, there is no other sound. The rain's stopped. Everything feels like it is happening in slow motion. Cinders fall as fiery rain.

Rex's eyes float to the doorway, the one Gus was ramming. The door is missing now, probably blown outwards. He knows what will happen next. Gus flies in, pinioning Charge to the brick wall in a bone-breaking tackle.

Rex makes a one-legged leap, as Gus's beak-mouth snaps through Charge's nose. Clearing them, Rex stumbles into the dreary twilight of outside, falling in the mud as far from the entrance as his strength will take him. He rolls on his back, gun held between legs and pointed at the open doorway. He hopes it still works.

The rising flames make a Halloween mask of the building's façade. Just on the pyre of sunset, a figure emerges, cloaked in flame and shrieking horribly. Rex cannot tell whether it is Gus or Charge.

He only has three bullets but is merciful.

The gun still works.

His mind is floating again. He finds himself in an unfamiliar memory. Looking round, he tries to describe the surroundings to himself in a couple of words. A room shaped like half a ribbed barrel. Hard tables with iron legs. Chairs, different makes and materials. Curtains pinned up to hide the iron walls and metal buttressing. On an old power box, candles in green glass chimneys. It is like someone has tried to prettify a … mess hall, perhaps. To convert it to … a makeshift restaurant? Rex tabulates the details, builds up the picture, but still he can't remember the place or locate himself in the picture. His unease grows.

Kerrie enters, wearing an elegant black number, with strapless back and plunging neckline. He never knew her to wear anything quite like that before. He'd always told her she could get away with clothes like that; now she must believe it herself. Her hair is pulled back, revealing all her face, and tizzed where it falls out in a bouffant flourish. A man appears behind her, whose identity is completely unknown to Rex. Tall, rakish. Skin, a deep brown, almost black. Jet, luxuriant hair, wavy. A thin moustache grown across the top of his lip, perfectly manicured. A cheeky, Errol Flynn type confidence. Lashes long and enviable. Too beautiful to be found on a man, he thinks jealously, pettily. Who is this hunk?

The matinee idol pulls out the wood and iron seat for Kerrie, a courtesy Rex never extended. She seems almost to curtsey, before sitting. The man finds his own seat after lightly brushing his hand across her exposed shoulders. The cheek! Rex tries to assert himself on the scene, make his presence felt, but in a frightening fashion, he can't seem to find himself to make that move.

The two radiate joy across the table and take each other's hands.

The man begins to speak in an Indian accent.

'I think I am old fashioned because I still believe in love. I believe healthy relationship is something you work at not something that happens – no? I love music and dancing …' the man winks lasciviously, '… except you need a partner. I love doing things outdoors, going to festivals, skiing, skydiving ...'

Rex stares uncomprehending. The scene is surreal, like a window onto a speed dating show. It doesn't make sense; none of this is memory to him.

He tunes back in.

'... you might think I'm reserved and shy at first ...' at this the man's look becomes saucy, '... but first impressions can be very misleading. I believe life is best lived with the glass spilling over, as opposed to half empty. For me, each day is a new adventure and I always look forward to tomorrow.'

Kerrie closes her eyes as she squeezes his hands. 'Go on.'

Rex feels a stab of grief. Oddly, all the ways in which this man describes himself are the opposite to Rex's personality. Is this some sort of indictment of him? A past infidelity on Kerrie's part? It can't be a present or future event. Could this scenario be of Rex's own imagining, a strange self-torture through holding up his inverse as a mocking censure?

Since the outbreak of the virus, his mind has become unchained, turning over past events in his life with a methodical, repetitive insistence.

But it was with an insistence he could mostly control. And, in his way, he liked it. Because he could revisit memories as he used to revisit the same select few places he photographed.

Some people make the mistake of believing that the best photography emerges out of chance. A chance shot of this, a serendipitous click of that. And, yes, the occasional great photograph does snap into existence in that way.

But in Rex's experience, and he believes the experience of the vast bulk of photographers, the opposite is true. The majority of great photography comes from visiting the same subjects, the same places, again and again, till you are intimate with their various, changing moods, how differing times of day light them up, till you are so intimate with them that that 'one shot', that serendipitous moment, is all the more likely to occur and be captured.

But as for this scene before him?

'No, it's not very easy finding someone to share your life with in time when divorce, cheating so high. Many many people do not believe they can find love because we live in a world where everything is instant. No one wants to work at things any more. But you can't hurry love and when you've got it, everything on your list and mine will not matter anymore. I am honest, caring, loving, understanding, have faith, nice guy to be very friendly. My ideal partner?'

'Please,' prompts Kerrie.

'My ideal partner would be same that I describe myself above or complementary. What we do in bed, each other's liking. And now, exquisite lady, you?'

Kerrie loses her relaxed countenance and dreamy eyelids. 'Please, I want to forget *me*.'

He protests but she clutches his hands. 'Please. I need to.' She blushes. 'Even if for a night.' She stands, he stands, and they lean over the table to kiss voraciously.

It's a strange scene, like the meeting he and Kerrie never had.

Rex comes to with tears in his eyes and rage in his heart.

He is still where he lay after shooting the fiery figure, the buildings burning around him.

Two shots.

CHAPTER SEVEN

Although covered in morning mist, Rex can see the desert is already sprinkled with fresh green and the beginnings of flowers, their buds craning to the rising sun. A feeling of exquisite, ineffable pain comes over him to see this explosion of new life, but he can at least partake by proxy in the joy of a land having drunk its fill. Kerrie suddenly seems infinitely remote, as if in this moment can be found a template for eternity. The wind ribbons his fingers. Silence is something we can't understand. Immediately the ineffable soundlessness is filled (as opposed to shattered) with the songs of birds launching from their nightly perches and winging it on the air.

He looks at the compound in the distance. The last of the flames and embers escape as spinning stars, spiralling out of the galaxy. He wasn't able to find

Crystal or Emmy's bodies. He hopes it was quick for them.

He stands stiffly, gauging the lay of the land. He might walk on a bit and enjoy the morning freshness before he shoots himself. Not even the hunger in his stomach can detract from the joy of the blossoming colour around him.

'Oh no ...'

He stares at the marks. Two sets of prints, and perhaps the tyre tracks of a trolley. One set of prints belongs to an adult, the other a child. It can only be them.

Why?

Why did they have to make it?

He feels a heaving disappointment it isn't over for them and, by extension, for himself. All the yawning adult responsibility caves back in, bringing with it an awareness of his aches and pains and bruises and hunger and thirst, making him feel vey human and tired once more. And heavy.

'Oh God, oh God.'

Stumbling, he follows the tracks.

'Gus, yeah, he danced in the rain, eh,' says Crystal, brushing her hair with a tortoiseshell comb. 'He reckoned they all knew somethin'. Somethin' 'bout all this. But they was just blind drunk and scary to me. We got outta there.'

Rex looks at the pram she filled with water and food. He calculates she's cached three days worth. Oh God. Three more days when he was ready now. Three of them and only two bullets in his gun.

Emmy takes his hand, and asks about the others.

Rex doesn't know how to tell them. Crystal gauges their fate from Rex's expression and ruffles Emmy's blonde bob.

'Thev moved to the next world, eh sweetheart.'

They walk for two hours, keeping to the highway they've found because it's easier with the pram. A triangular, yellow sign indicates a lookout ahead. They walk off the road and up to the balconied barricade over the vast plain before them. Clouds tug their shadows across the expanse. The world steps off the horizon. A thread of river, the road, and a town beyond. And flowing amongst all that salt and pepper land, great cursive swathes of stone, the creator's anagram. They realise they have come to a saddle of rock between two crests of the Bactrian mountain.

Following the zigzag road down, their gate becomes their own ocean. With Emmy atop Rex's shoulders, she becomes her own ship.

Crystal talks about the food she misses as she wheels their squeaky pram half full of food that doesn't really go together.

'Loved me KFC. Sure as shit miss that shit. Salt and

sugar – miss 'em so much. Charge, he loiked Chinese takeaway. Sweet and sour pork – he fucken loved that.'

Rex laughs, half in madness.

She slows and squints at him. 'Yeah?'

He stops. 'Nothing.'

They walk on, Emmy slipping down onto Rex's back and promptly falling asleep. Crystal stops to put a red scarf under her straw hat, letting the back out to cover her brown neck and shoulders.

'Yeah, he loiked a lot of Asian stuff. Their filums, karate, food … girls.'

'There was a lot that was very silly about our world,' he says, at last finding the strength to be glad they're still alive.

She finishes fiddling with her hat and scarf and pushes on. 'Yeah, sure as shit was.'

Rex can only admire that she is still attentive to her dress. He looks down at his grubby, ash and mud-stained clothes and promises when they stop he'll scrub up fit for a funeral.

In a rest-spot, they find a Mazda, and something about it makes Rex think of family drives when he was young. This one is mustard yellow, though; his family's beetle green, from memory. He tries the door and finds it unlocked. Even more surprising, the key's in the ignition. He turns the engine over and it starts. Not much petrol but maybe enough to get them twenty, thirty kilometres further down the road. He wonders briefly about its last occupants, but there is nothing to give away their personalities.

Planning to drive it in the morning, they head into the bush to find somewhere scenic to camp.

A cleft of rock where a great boulder has fallen down above, wedging in tight halfway to form something of a ceiling, makes the grade. The tent erected and bedding laid out, Rex volunteers to fetch wood.

'I wanna come!'

'Yeah, go on then,' says Crystal, busy about dinner, working the disparate ingredients into something palatable.

Rex and Emmy wander through the pillared cloister of the trees, the leaves still moist from the downpour. It's overcast, and without light to model the trees' shapes, the whole scene could be a damp, wool tapestry.

Rex finds himself silently lecturing. There are three ways of separating a subject from its background in photography. One, through depth: the subject in focus, the background out. Two, through colour: preferably contrasting rather than complimentary (the stunning red of a cyclamen against the green of ferns, say). Three, through light: the subject lit, the background in darkness. And sometimes vice versa, if you want a silhouette.

Rex looks round at the uniformity of damp dull green and grey and knows he would have been hard-pressed to get a good shot here.

But then his head comes in line with a purple leaf, bumpy with beads of water, hanging against a tangle of white moss, and he changes his mind.

He takes a photo with his eyes, the image forever burned on his retinas, then kneels and reaches for a dryish log on the ground.

A shape flits past, then another. They are … dogs! Rex quickly rises. Large dogs. *Only* large dogs. Of course, they probably ate the little ones. He steps towards one, a Beagle.

'Here, boy.'

It growls.

'Hey, I'm just saying …'

It's joined by a third, a fourth, a fifth, a … hunting pack.

Rex drops his bundles of sticks.

'Emmy, take my hand.'

'Where's Soldia?'

He tells her to discard her armful of kindling.

There are at least three more, still keeping their distance. He pulls Emmy in close. What about Crystal? He edges in the direction of their camp. There's a sixth, which looks like an Alsatian. Flanking them from a distance, its eyes seem fixed on Emmy.

'Stay close, Em.'

The little girl's eyes grow wide and she starts to

cry; he berates himself for letting his fear show in his voice. He pointlessly feels for the gun in his pocket but knows from its absent weight he left it at the camp. The Doberman and Great Dane draw closer, followed by the Staffordshire Bull Terrier. The variegated Staffy still has a collar and a chain dragging from its neck.

'Stay … stay …'

From the way their ears pitch, the words are evidently familiar to them, but they're lean, hungry. Food first.

If the pack's here, Crystal must be safe. Unless they already got her? No, he would have heard. Getting torn apart by dogs would be noisy …

What can he do? Hoist Emmy up a tree? But then what? Won't that prolong her demise, if he's then taken?

He turns slightly, not wanting to show his back to the leader. But where's that Alsatian …? He swivels as it leaps at him.

Rex falls, cradling Emmy. He feels retracted claws and slobbering. The others race in. The Alsatian growls – at them!

Rex sits up as they all back off, except the Alsatian.

'*Buzz* …?' cries Rex, astounded.

Buzz whines with joy.

'Buzz! It's okay, Emmy, this is Buzz, my other dog.'

He shakes her thick mane, looking into her deep black eyes. 'Oh, Buzz!'

Buzz whines and wiggles and licks and slobbers.

He holds her face away for a moment. 'Roger? Where's Roger?'

Buzz doesn't move. This was the dog that travelled three suburbs and found Roger after he bolted from hot air balloons. She doesn't go sniffing this time; she must know his fate. Poor dim Roger, who'd crouch before a tree root, expecting Rex to throw it. He was dead before Rex and Kerrie even made it down their cellar. But Buzz … what a dog.

'Can I pat?'

'Yes, Em,' he says.

Rex turns to the other dogs. 'Sit!' he barks at the Staffy. It sits. Rex reaches out a hand and it … *he*, Rex notes … sniffs. Rex looks at the collar once he's removed it.

'Bunny!'

On their way back, they pass a lame sheep struggling, lagging behind its flock. The dogs surge forward with intent. Buzz looks to Rex. He covers Emmy's eyes and whispers, 'Go get.'

He pushes Emmy ahead, telling her he'll catch her up, then turns back to watch the dogs tear into the sheep, their old hierarchy re-established in the orgy of eating. The smell and sight of blood and flesh make them salivate.

After his, Crystal's and Emmy's meal, the pack joins them. Buzz, throat bloodied, puts a proprietorial paw on Rex's knee. Leaning forward to scratch behind Buzz's silken ears, Rex recognises with a start a contented feeling in his gut. Is this happiness? Bellies full, they all settle to sleep, the dogs comfortable in the companionship of friendly humans and the warmth of their fire, a luxury till now they'd almost forgotten.

He wakes in the night. A firm decision.

'We've got to get in the car, Crystal,' he whispers.

Crystal removes the tattered butterfly sleep mask she'd found somewhere and sits up, rubbing her eyes.

'Eh, what, why?'

Buzz keeps pace for a good few hundred metres as they drive off, the dust making her look like a ghost. Oh God, how his heart hurts. But they're dead and she still has a chance.

Their last campsite. This time, situated on flats edged with a temporary lake. Like the night before, Rex and Emmy grub for wood, Crystal having insisted she'd cook.

He and Emmy find an old sandstone house with the ceiling caved in, and gather the bone white timber under their arms. Emmy is faster, talkative, telling Rex how she could make this place into a real-life doll's house; Rex is mute, and feeble in his foraging. He can't get his energy up. His heart is empty from having to say goodbye to Buzz twice … And then there was Kerrie, Kerrie with that guy. Where were the two dining? Looked like army barracks made up to be 'nice'. Was she seeing him? And why wasn't *he*, Rex, in the scene? How could he remember something he wasn't involved in?

Crystal appears at an empty window frame.

'Here.'

She places a bottle of black-label whisky under his nose, on the stone lintel.

'Managed to hide it from them soaks back there. Bin savin' it for yers …' She laughs. 'Savin' it for what, I wanna know!'

Crystal notes Rex's glum face, then tunes into Emmy's unceasing discourse.

'Wan' a minute alone?'

Rex nods thanks. Crystal helps Emmy with the firewood. Rex watches mother and daughter walk back to the camp, the little girl struggling under the weight of the firewood. Perhaps they should finish it tonight? Get a bit drunk but not too drunk that he'll miss. But two shots …? He won't tell Crystal that. He'll shoot Emmy, then Crystal, then … what to do with himself? Drink water?

He wanders to the farther wall of the house, which has toppled outward at knee height, and sits on the stone. He swigs the whisky. Not being used to it and with his leaner shape, the alcohol hits him hard. The sun stretches across the long grass; everything is tinged with a brownish red. Cold is settling in. He looks over at the already roaring fire Emmy and Crystal have made. They are playing lightsabre battles with half burnt sticks, the sparks flying whenever they make contact. He'll join them in a moment, share the whisky.

He tenderly appraises her when Kerrie sits down next to him, and watches the scene he's watching. She's wearing a tuxedo blazer paired with jeans and strappy sandals. He doesn't want to bring up the subject (what does it matter now if she had an affair?) but can't help himself.

'Who was the guy?' he asks.

She stares at him, confused.

'Suresh – the Bollywood heartthrob.'

Her face flushes in pain. 'But …? How …? You're there, even then? You can't even give me that?'

The anger he pretended wasn't there, makes itself flagrant and he curses her. She could at least be contrite, embarrassed, anything but annoyed with *him*.

Kerrie is ashen during his tirade. When he flags, she asks quietly, her eyes cast down, 'Did you watch us … while we …?'

They stare at the fire, its light jiggling in the hunched trees and on the animated faces of Crystal and Emmy, deep in conversation.

'What were we doing?' asks Kerrie. 'When I'd get

home to whinge about my research, you your lack of success in photography – we could have lived.'

'We'll all be dead soon,' he says. 'We all will be. And that will be an achievement of sorts. We can rest.'

He reconsiders. Will they? Kerrie is an unquiet ghost.

'Who will you be with *then*, Rex? Who? Me or Crystal?'

He can't say.

'Rex?'

He still can't say.

'What have I done?' moans Kerrie.

Rex trips, stumbles and falls, because ... Because how can one love, really love, more than one partner?

Ain't nobody

Loves me better.

He feels for the first time Kerrie's fear. How can someone who's truly loved me, love another – *better*? Ain't nobody. There ain't nobody.

Rex is at that table with his father in the backyard of the café, the furniture as convincing as a stage setting, the garden and fence behind them as real as painted flats.

His father sees him reading *A History of Torture*.

'Why, Rex?'

Rex puts the book cover-down on the table.

'I want to know.'

'You should also read a history of art.'

Rex flips the book to look at its cover. He envies his father's balance.

'In a way I feel for you young'uns,' says his father, cigarette stuck with saliva to his bottom lip. 'It seems like you have more opportunity and choice, but you don't. And there's no longer a clear demarcation between when childhood ends and adulthood begins.'

His father pulls the cigarette from its perch on his lip, the skin tenting momentarily.

The scene dismantles before Rex, his father and the backyard fading, leaving Rex in contemplative darkness.

He is brought back to the present, to his perch atop the half-collapsed sandstone wall.

What would his father have done at the beginning of this train of events? His father would have stopped Kerrie. His father worked tirelessly, endlessly, with good cheer. He never felt … self-pity. He never felt … special.

'A ghost?' asks Kerrie, next to him.

He nods. 'But a ghost you can feel. I hope Soldier feels me by her side from time to time.'

'What did Gary do,' asks Kerrie, 'when he tore the delicate membrane separating our universe from its cousins? If there are an infinite number of universes–'

' – hanging on the wall,' he butts in, resorting to nursery rhyme, the way they had when they first met.

'An infinite number of universes, hanging on the wall,' she continues.

'And one such universe should accidentally fall?'

'Then somewhere – *somewhere*, Rex – there exists our exact counterparts, sitting like mismatched birds as we are now. Somewhere, we made it. Somewhere, we're happy.'

Rex realises she has more she wants to say, and this time refrains from interrupting.

'Rex, I don't know why I wanted success so much. My parents didn't force me to want to be the best, to stand out. Why? I finally understand your dream to tread lightly. When my research became top secret, I regretted the absence of accolades. Like you said, there should be prizes for people who make the least impact on the world. What we could have had.'

'Is this you, Kerrie?' asks Rex. 'I hope so. I hope we're finally together.'

'You should have stopped me.'

'I know. I shouldn't have wanted to disappear so completely. I should have stood out.'

'For the right reasons.'

She pulls her blazer in closer, buttoning it. Cold?

'How will I ever let go of you, Rex?' she exults – sadly. 'To live with what Oppenheimer lived with – multiplied a million fold. That's me.'

He joins Crystal and Emmy in a strangely buoyant mood, the alcohol and conversation with Kerrie having calmed him. Emmy is rocking in Crystal's arms.

'Yous talking to her again?'

Rex double-takes. But Crystal can only mean one person. He nods, before fetching three cups. He pours them all whiskies after asking if it's all right to give Emmy a thimbleful.

He pulls up a wet log and sits. Crystal and Emmy stare at him. Was that what mother and daughter were talking about so earnestly, Rex's chinwags with Kerrie? Crystal won't elaborate. The three share a desultory meal together.

When they've finished, he tries to get Crystal talking. He likes it when she gets into full flow, because she will cover topics of comforting familiarity: Christmas shopping, paintball excursions she and her mates would go on, all-time favourite pub gigs. But right now, he can't nudge her, no matter how hard he tries.

He feels angry that she's squandering the gift of whisky. So much for making this their last night.

'Come on, then, at least tell me some of the things you and Emmy would do.'

'Make play-dough crocs,' says Emmy.

Rex encourages Emmy instead but the poor girl trails off without her mother's participation, and is soon asleep, the effects of the tiny amount of alcohol taking their toll. His own voice becoming as obnoxious to him as in a library or church, he too resorts to silence.

The only sounds left are the critters in the bush, and the water popping in the green branches they've thrown onto the fire. Neither he nor Crystal tend to it. The flames gradually die down till they're almost in darkness. When she at last speaks, he can no longer see her face.

'You wouldna looked two ways at me if all this 'adn't 'appen, eh?'

Rex stops kicking at the fire. Ah, so *that's* what's upsetting her.

He beams but then realises she can't see his expression and relocates the warmth to his voice.

'Hey, there's a lot I wouldn't have done,' he says. 'Not all of it bad.'

He shuffles over and puts his arms around her and Emmy. Who was he kidding to think he'd end it tonight for them? True to character, he was always going to wait till the last possible moment.

Morning. They set out for their last trek, with their food and water for one final day transferred to backpacks, the pram abandoned by the lake. Crystal tells Rex they've known each other for ten weeks. She finds meaning in the roundness of that number. They survey the prospect of their last hike: an epiphany of rocks and ranges, hidden caves and spectacular gorges, dominant bluffs and bold breakaways, all lit up with colour, the desert alive with colour from that monsoonal downpour. They couldn't have chosen a better outing to end their lives.

They walk among serried rows of startling pink dwarf swainsona; brush past fussy branches of spearbush popping with bell-shaped creamy flowers; catch their clothes on grevillea in its multitude of colours, from red to orange to green; and step carefully among pink and yellow daisies.

They walk between marble gums, witchetty bush and mulga trees, and the ubiquitous spinifex grass.

They draw in the scent of the sweet smelling cassias, erupting in their yellow flowers.

While meantime, everywhere there are birds. Bee-eaters from New Guinea, crimson chats, cockatiels, budgerigars, button quails. Black, white and pied honeyeaters. Migrating water birds (sandpipers) and black-tailed godwits. Also, birds of prey: black falcons, little eagles.

They climb a skerry of rocks to see a plain of muddy earth carpeted in heath myrtle, alive with its combination of pink and white flowers. Growing amid them, the desert fuchsia, equally colourful. And in bands of striated colour, succulents like the purple parakeelyas.

It's a grand day to die.

'Look, look!' squeals Emmy.

They look, and can't believe their eyes. Four elephants, a picture of family: a bull, cow, and their two calves, emerging from behind a stand of Acaccia.

'Ephalents! Ephalents!' shouts Emmy.

'They must have been freed from a zoo,' marvels Rex, secretly hoping there is another survivor out there, who cares for animals as he does.

The herd is a couple of hundred metres distant, moving away from them.

Smiles ricochet between Rex and Crystal at both the incongruous site before them, and the unending commentary from Emmy. A vision, perhaps, gifted to them on their day of passing, of inextinguishable life. Perhaps not human, but glorious in its resilience.

They follow the elephants at a distance to see them enter a town.

Ten minutes later, they enter that town themselves, with its wide horizontals (roofs, verandas, curbs), and short verticals (street signs, posts, poles) and it strikes Rex how easy the proverbial Aussie country town has been for painters. Brown coat over white, the spatula used to gouge away the lines. Dobs of green here, squares of black or white there, all against the wash of a blue sky.

This town could be an Australian town at any other time except that the blobs on this impressionist piece have extra details on closer view. Yawning windows with smashed glass teeth; a gutter half off, a rare line of incline; and a bin rolling drunkenly in the wind, its contents long vomited up.

A flapping awning over a butcher's shop sparks in Rex a pastel vision of a country town of colour and friendship, with men tipping their hats, woman gossiping good-naturedly, kids playing unwatched. Was that idealised memory of small town country life ever real to anyone?

Was there ever a time when life was tender? When love was plentiful, and hate lay fallow? When enough was not more than anyone should ever own, but all that we could need?

They enter the main drag, and the sky erupts in waving gloves, before being thrown down as they pass as if in challenge. Birds. In an eerie homage to the film and novella before it, they perch and gabble on every surface, their black-and-white graffiti neither washed off by human hands nor recent rain. Their tap dancing on the roofs, either metallic or a clinking, depending on corrugated or clay, forms an arrhythmic chorus.

Rex and Crystal pull Emmy in close between them.

Movement. Three kangaroos: large reds. Rex and Crystal laugh aloud for no reason other than the sheer pleasure of the sight. Kangaroos hopping down suburban streets – it's exactly the sort of picture that many foreigners nurture of Australia, a notion once so rare in fact as to be virtually false, but now fabulously true! Rex is happy for all the creatures that will now thrive. He's happy in a more generous spirit than he was when he'd intellectualised humankind's passing.

At the end of the street, palms rise up over the low buildings, their crowns like lit fuses. They approach closer, to find the palms are part of the town's botanical gardens. Skipping over the flattened iron entrance gates, again they see the elephants, but this time writ large, picking fruit among the introduced trees. He's never been this close to an elephant before. Not without a fence or sides of a safari bus between them. And they're big. The noise they make as they eat, their snorting breath, the thwacking of their tatty ears against their heads. Elephants with their sad expressions, playing. Trunks – now snail's shells, now canes swung just above the ground. Now held up to pluck. Hides, the colour of rock. Small eyes, but deep.

Emmy steps forward, accidentally kicking a bottle. It spins, eventually coming to rest, its open end pointing at Rex. The bottle doesn't break but its clink is resounding. The herd immediately shies, a short trumpet sounding from the bull.

They take Emmy's hand and step back.

'Bewdy-ful,' says Crystal.

Rex can only repeat the sentiment before the tableau of their own family mimicked in these magnificent beasts.

His breathless joy at the scene buoys him up with a feeling of reverence he's never felt before. Old thoughts about digitally capturing the beauty before him lie dormant. He wonders if he isn't finally before his altar.

He's drawn into their eyes, their sad profile eyes, as each views him in their ascending landscape. But just as he is used to reading from left to right, so too do his eyes keep returning to that of the elephant in front, the female matriarch.

He always wondered at the poet's obsession with an organ that, on its own, he felt was not as expressive as given credit for. But here, even with the other features somewhat vignetted in his mind, he is intoxicated by a very real and expressive eloquence in that eye.

And what that eye is eloquent of just now can be reduced to one word.

Memory.

Memory of humans.

Of just what humans are like ...

He stumbles back.

With another trumpet, the bull, cow, and calves swing round to face them.

'Run!' shouts Rex.

He turns, but Crystal and Emmy are still enraptured.

'Run!' he hollers again, half-hoisting Emmy, Crystal catching on and copying his move as the elephants charge.

The sound of the stampeding on the bitumen, a

building drum roll to an impending crescendo.

Even as Rex runs from the garden entrance, he understands that this is what the elephants must do. They won't make it with humans still in the picture and even as he fears the encroaching pain, he approves the intended act.

They duck under the veranda of the Mayoral Office, the bull throwing its trunk under as they scrabble at the door. It is joined by the cow and they each lasso a post. The sound of wood splintering and metal tearing intermingles with their trumpeting. The posts give way, the veranda collapsing just as Rex, Crystal and Emmy get the door open and bundle inside.

They make their way out the back, to an alley. The bull is waiting and charges. They run the opposite way but their path is blocked by an abandoned Ford Festiva. Rex gets the boot open and they climb inside and through the back seats. Rex just gets himself inside when the bull rears up, then crashes down on the boot, the rear window exploding like a fountain that's suddenly turned on.

Crystal is trying to kick out the front windscreen. The bull steps on the boot. As the bonnet flicks up, the front screen pops. Rex pushes them through the hole only to discover that the cow has blocked their way.

He has no choice but to bring out the gun, aiming directly between her eyes. At the last second he lifts his hand. The sound is enough to make her shy away. But that's Crystal's bullet gone now. Only one left, for Emmy.

Crystal is already on the bonnet and pushing Crystal up the drainpipe of the adjoining building. Rex pushes her up next. He leaps himself off his one good foot as the cow and bull close back in. He rolls onto the roof as their trunks flap over the sides like grey tentacles.

He ventures a look into the alley and reads their expressions. Memory. They're not going to let them go at that. He watches a moment as each elephant begins to slowly back out opposite ends of the alley, and realises they still have time for escape.

'Run!'

Crystal picks up Emmy and races up a slanted green-glass roof.

'Not, not that – '

The roof gives way beneath mother and daughter. Rex hears a thud followed a split-second later by a splash.

Frantically looking down through the broken glass, he watches Crystal's head emerge from a lake of scum, from what must be the public indoor swimming pool. Emmy is flat on her back on the diving board, looking for all the world like a discarded doll. She's motionless.

Rex quickly leans over and throws his gun to the side of the pool, hoping that despite the sound it didn't break. He holds his nose and jumps.

Not till he's out of the water does he even open his eyes. Crystal has made it out before him and is spluttering on the aqua tiles.

Rex swiftly checks on Emmy before grabbing the handgun (which seems intact) and returning to Crystal and holding her in his arms. He knows from her spluttering what will come next, and the look on her face confirms she knows too.

'Oi swallowed some.'

Her eyes find Emmy, legs and arms hanging loose either side of the diving board, and she tries to scrabble towards her. Rex holds her back.

'She's safe now,' he whispers. 'Emmy's safe from this world now. She's gone to the next.'

'Couldn't save er, could oi?'

Crystal clutches at his arm. Already her face is twitching. 'Yous said this was it with you, Rex? Is it?'

Rex holds her close. 'No,' he says. 'There's something else.' He quickly tells her, knowing this is no time to play games. 'I looked around at the world and despaired before I had anything to despair of. I despaired before I knew what I was losing. And I found my courage only when you and Emmy gave me hope.'

'Weakness.'

He nods.

'Shoot me.'

He lifts the gun, holding the barrel at her temple.

'One shot?' she says, concern for him. How did she know?

He shrugs like it doesn't matter. Her face twitches, her mouth curls at the corners, up at one end, down at the other, a happy/sad clown.

He sings, 'Ain't nobody – '

' – loves me better,' she finishes urgently.

'Makes me happy, makes me feel this … ' And he lets her complete the line.

'… way.' Her word deteriorates to a growl.

'Ain't nobody …'

She drools. He shoots.

He shoots.

Ain't nobody.

Kerrie is standing near him. But not beside him. Maybe in death no one belongs to anyone anymore. He feels that's better.

He has moved Emmy to the showers recess, and sits there, stroking her hair.

Great shadows pass back and forth against the tinted green of the entrance windows. They're waiting for him, and Rex can only admire the wisdom of their grim fortitude.

But he's not dead yet and he always wanted to determine the manner and timing of his own parting.

Rex smashes through the maintenance door in the cleaning buggy, its brushes whirring either side,

Emmy bundled on the back. He hopes the two hours he spent shedding it of extraneous weight have made it faster. He hears the elephants lumbering from the front to intercept him. Reaching the main street, he already has a good few hundred metres on them. They charge, even the calves joining in the stampede. The birds erupt from the rooves like synchronised fountains, one going off after the other.

Rex once feels a trunk brush against his back but knows this time he's made it.

He drives till the battery fails and the cleaning buggy putters to a stop, reaching as far as the outskirts of town. He picks up Emmy and walks down to a river, and gently lays her on the sand.

He paces.

'Why are you walking like that?' she asks.

He turns to Kerrie.

'I'm trying to miss the ants.'

Kerrie chokes back a sob. 'Oh, Rex.'

'Treading lightly,' he affirms.

He reaches down to feel Emmy's pulse. He'd lied to Crystal. Emmy wasn't dead; she was simply knocked out. He lifts her up. She wakes groggily.

'Where's Mummy?'

'Your Mummy's gone to the next world. We're joining her.'

'How?'

'Through playing a game. We need to collect all

the smooth pebbles.'

Emmy helps him pick out the pebbles from the water's edge then complains they lose their wonderful colours once exposed to air.

He agrees, filling his pockets with them.

'My turn.'

'Sure.'

She fills hers.

'I'm getting heavy, Daddy Rex.'

'Come into the water with me, Em. You'll feel lighter.'

He loops his belt to hers.

They splash in the water.

'It's okay to drink it now, Emmy.'

She gives him a funny look. He pretends to drink first.

'You only pretended to drink, Daddy Rex!'

Christ, this isn't going to be easy. Why is it getting harder, not easier, for him to kill? But that's a good thing, surely?

With the recent rain, the current's strong. He pushes them out, still holding onto her waist. His feet dance in the mud and rocks.

'Aren't you thirsty, Em?'

'Where's Dad?' she asks, surprising him. Can she mean Charge?

His feet are lifted off the bottom; they're taken by the current.

'You miss him?'

'Yes, but you're importanter.'

They pass by a snag. Rex grabs it but can feel the weight and water bringing them down, their clothes now sodden.

'You can drink now,' he says.

Emmy's face contorts with fear.

'I wanna go back.'

She tries to swim. He pulls her under. Oh God, oh God. She struggles in his arms. She comes up, face in terror, spluttering.

'You swallowed some?'

She bites her lip.

'It's okay if you did.'

She nods.

Rex waits till he thinks he sees her face twitching before letting go of the snag. Going under, the water gets in his mouth as he kicks and struggles.

So many thoughts crowd in on him, so many moments, which are big moments in hindsight. On his eighth birthday, a cake his mother made in the shape of a volcano, its hollowed out centre filled with chuckling red jelly. Cavorting with friends on a beach at sixteen, finding round a bluff the source of the smell that had already announced itself: the half rotting carcass of a whale, its ribcage the rarely seen skeleton of a wave. At twenty-seven, an all muscle-and-sinew homeless man, tanned like hide, watches how far down to the filter Rex will smoke his cigarette before giving it up to the ground.

Of what import such recollections when mortal? As consciousness escapes his own grasp, a final question:

If we'd seen the future as unchangeable as the past, what would we have made of now?

CHAPTER EIGHT

Rex hears before he sees: a plane flying low. He opens his eyes. There is a beach. A beach seems right, so appropriately *right* somehow, even if the beach is on a riverbank. He lifts his head to better scope his surroundings, then rolls on his back. Emmy is making a sloppy sand castle. He coughs up river water. Is she dead? They're dead, yes? They both drank the water. He rolls to the gently lipping water of the river and cups a handful to his mouth.

'It's okay,' says Emmy. 'Tastes yummy.'

Rex drinks. He feels for the virus rising in him. Nothing. She's right: it's yummy, and it's life. Now what?

'Rex?'

He turns to her.

'The plane flewed over. Will they rescue us?'

Rex remembers he heard it himself and stares open-mouthed.

They head in the direction Emmy said the plane was flying. It was very low by her account, so he figures it must have been coming in to land, and that means somewhere relatively close. Trekking through scrub, they happen upon a road that rolls up to what looks like an unmanned military guard station with raised boom-gate. There is a jeep, clean, functioning, parked next to the guard booth. Knowing how to dismantle a steering column, Rex hotwires it and drives off-road to an isolated spot. He sneaks the last of the whisky into Emmy's drink. She's out pretty quick. He figures he has an hour before she wakes.

He walks back to the road, pulling branches across to conceal the spot he went off-road.

He jogs along the bitumen.

It leads to a similarly unmanned fence, wide open.

Beyond, a chequerboard of soldiers' huts, recently erected, judging from the sheen of their paintjobs. Rex sees movement and ducks behind a dormitory wall. Peering out, a formation of soldiers marches by in camouflage, guns resting against shoulders. He follows them at a distance. Soon he comes upon a square, filled with military personnel at their business, and a landing strip beyond with several planes. A flag is being raised in the centre dais.

Is it American?

As it is hoisted up, he is brought down, descending into despair.

The red, white and blue.

'Oh God, oh God,' he beats the ground. 'Why did we have to make it? The world could have lived without us. The world could live without us.'

On his way out, he sees a smartly dressed woman enter one of the fancier prefabricated dwellings. Wait, that unmistakable figure and gait ... How? It can't be ...

Following her inside, he passes by an open bedroom door, and pauses. There is a man asleep, a twisted white sheet failing to hide his modesty. The man groans, rolls on his front. Rex feels a shock of recognition, but not from life ... from dream.

Suresh, the man with whom he saw Kerrie dine then make love.

A voice, crystal and real, comes from the kitchen, judging by the echo.

'You getting up, sleepyhead?'

Rex darts back from the bedroom door then makes his way to the kitchen.

She jumps back, her voice shaking: 'Rex ...?'

'Kerrie?'

Again, she is wearing something different. This time it is the khaki of army dress. It seems in bad taste for a ghost.

For the first time, an unreality that should have

accompanied his other meetings with Kerrie's ghost, descends upon him.

Kerrie is the first to manage a sentence.

'I … I dream about you. You haunt my dreams. Oh God, how you haunt them … But this? How is *this* possible?'

'I don't know,' says Rex, trying to calm himself and her. 'But I thought you'd be used to it.'

Kerrie trembles. 'In my dreams, yes. But, Rex, right now I'm … *awake*.'

It is Rex's turn to stumble, stopping moments before her, his hands outstretched. He feels his colour drain out. She answers the question in his expression.

'We found your body, Rex.'

His stomach free-falls. 'In the river?'

She signals confusion. 'No. The cellar.'

He can only parrot her. 'The cellar …?'

Rex feels a strange turning, the room turning. 'We went down there together,' he insists.

A spinning.

'No, Rex. I came back to the house for you. I tried to get you to join me at the bunker.'

'But the virus broke out at the bunker,' he rejoins, dizzy.

'Yes …' she says slowly. 'When we returned we saw that, but there was a helicopter waiting for us. I begged you, I begged you to come.'

Rex gets hold of the room and stares at her. 'And

why … wouldn't I?'

Her top lip twists up in momentary hatred, and he suddenly knows, and can answer himself. 'I wouldn't leave my dogs.'

His hands tremble, his hands that tried to drown Emmy.

'But … but I've been wandering, Kerrie, meeting other people. Crystal, Emmy, Charge … Malcolm!'

'Malcolm …? *He* died in the base, Rex.'

'How?'

She shakes her head. Were they other lost souls, making their way up the planes of limbo towards salvation? He thinks of Jenny and their last conversation before she headed out to search for the gun.

'Hey,' he called out before she could slip through the door. 'You really believe we keep living over our lives till we get them right?'

She managed a quarter smile. 'Yes, you've still got centuries to redeem yourself.'

Jenny had passed out of that room, that existence, to … another one? The multiverse?

The drifting in and out of moments in his life, the reliving of them, all the lives they could have had.

'Oh God, Kerrie, I'm trapped in limbo. Oh God.'

She starts to wail. 'What are we going to do?'

He stops moaning, gets a grip on himself.

'The water?' asks Rex. 'Can you steam it to kill the virus?'

She nods, frowning. 'Of course. We always could.'

Then ...?

A flashback to his father, his father hinting. 'What is the definition of hell, Rex? To suffer perpetual thirst.'

He holds Kerrie's eye, a fear for his soul in his chest. 'I'm in hell.'

'Limbo, surely,' she moans.

He paces, trying to think. He can drink the water now, so maybe he has moved out of hell. He thinks about Emmy. Can people grow up in limbo? He needs to get back to her (she's something he can hold onto) and takes a step towards the door.

Kerrie screams, distraught. 'Don't leave me!'

Suresh mumbles something from the bedroom.

Rex hesitates. Until now, he'd decided the most plausible explanation for this drifting back and forth through moments in time was that Gary had weakened the cell walls of the muliverse, allowing that ultimate virus, the human mind, to escape and multiply. Maybe that was still true?

Kerrie steps towards him.

'Rex, all these dreams about you – I thought that was me unable to let go of you. Well, I still think that. You, it was always you, Rex.'

Her skin is jewelled with tiny beads of sweat.

'What about Suresh?' he asks at last.

She winces. 'He's lovely. But he's lost his special someone too.'

He glances back down the corridor, past the bedroom door to the open front door. Emmy will wake soon. And if she wakes up alone ... He flicks his head back to Kerrie.

'Kerrie, if I can save this one girl, I'll come back for you.'

She understands from their shared dreams. 'Emmy?'

'Yes, babe. If we have more than one shot, I'll let you know.'

She falls on the floor. 'Please.'

'I must, Kerrie. You see, with Emmy I've finally realised: I want the world to be a better place.'

She sobs uncontrollably. 'Go. I'll follow.'

She rushes to a pile of military clothes (Suresh's?) thrown over a chair, reveals a holster under a camouflage jacket, and withdraws its gun. She holds the barrel to her temple.

'No, not that way!' and his hands pass through hers. For the first time, he realises how much he misses her touch. They try to grip each other, fumbling, passing through, him through her and her through him, each crying.

'Let me end this, Rex,' she sobs.

For a moment, he can't find a reason to stop her.

'Well, and what about Suresh in there?' he answers at last. 'He's given you comfort when you needed it. You've comforted each other. Would you leave him now, after that?'

She draws in a tortured breath. 'How can someone love more than one person? Who will we be with in the afterlife?'

'I've a feeling no one will own anyone or anything,' says Rex, a slow smile lighting his features.

Because he feels this one certitude at last. Whether his present state is the result of Gary's meddlings with the structure of time/space, or Rex has tapped into an already underlying 'wheel of life', he knows either way: there is a point to everything after all.

'Kerrie,' he says gently, 'do what you can to undo what we've done.'

'And when it's over?' she asks.

He walks to the door, and turns.

'I'll be back for you, Kerrie. This time you can know I'll be there for you. Heaven is a place on earth – we just have to make that true.'

Good, Emmy's still asleep in the front passenger seat. Rex backs up the jeep to the road where he's already pulled aside the concealing branches. He then sticks the gear in first, driving up to the guard house.

Emmy wakes. 'Where we going, Daddy Rex?'

'To find Buzz.'

'But, but, but, how?'

'I don't know,' he laughs then, as he passes under the raised boom-pole, spots a jerry can leaning against the booth. He stops the jeep and gets out to fetch it.

'Kiss,' says Emmy.

Rex goes to her window, where she's winding it all the way down. 'But I'm only going over there,' he clowns.

'*Kiss.*'

The photographer recalls the few photographs he's been in himself. He's always been in the back row, or a shadowy figure half out of shot. Now he wishes he could go back and be the star. He abrogated his responsibility to live, to question, to matter.

He thinks of the shadow of life, of television, the flimsiest impression of life, of how much we miss. Of how we're misled. What's wrong with him?

He mentally slaps himself. Wake up, wake up to life! He wants to stand out, to matter. He wants to say of life, I'll give it my best, I'll play my part, I won't be selfish, I'll start now. *Today*. A shame. How we let ourselves be the background to our own lives. He leans through the window and kisses her on the cheek.

'I'm here now, Emmy. You don't have to worry any more, darling, because … Yes, because – because I'm here! I'm finally, finally here.'

the end

ONE SHOT